CW00486505

Everyone's a Winner

Copyright © 2019 by Beth Pipe
All text and photographs

All map images taken from © OpenStreetMap contributors. Available under the Open Database Licence
http://www.openstreetmap.org/copyright

A series of short stories based in real Cumbrian towns and villages, because not all amazing locations are fictional.

CONTENTS

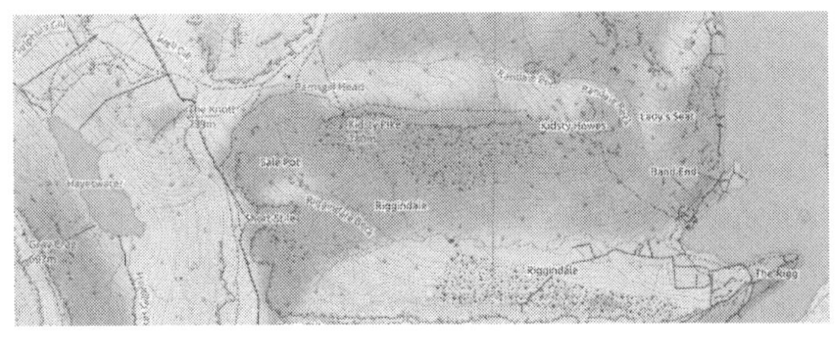

HIKERS IN THE MIST

"That's not Haweswater."

"Sorry?"

"I said, that's not Haweswater." Suzy pointed down through a break in the clouds to a lake far below.

John stood still for a moment, craning his head first one way then the other. She was right, it definitely wasn't Haweswater. "So where is it then?"

Suzy dug the map out and they both studied it. "My best guess is it's Hayeswater"

"It kinda sounds the same, is it far from Haweswater?"

"Not as the crow flies, but we're not crows."

"An astute observation so, where are we then?"

"Grey Crag. When we went to the cairn on Racecourse Hill we must have turned ourselves around somehow. I thought it didn't feel right, but I can't see anything in this damned mist."

"OK, what are our options?"

Suzy moved her glasses down her nose so she could peer over them to see the map more clearly. "Well we only really have one option – drop down off the end of the crag, cross the footbridge at the bottom, then climb back up over The Knott and down Kidsty Pike like we originally planned, but time is against us."

John looked at his watch. "We should have at least another couple of hours of daylight left, shouldn't we?"

"Don't forget the clocks went back last night, it'll be dark just after 6 o'clock, which gives us an hour tops."

"Oh."

"Yes. Oh." Suzy slipped her backpack off her shoulders, put it on the floor in front of her and began going through the pockets.

"What are you looking for?"

"My headtorch."

"Erm..."

"What do you mean, 'erm'?"

"I used it last week to put the bins out. I think it's still on my desk."

Suzy glared at him. "Do you ever put anything back where it's supposed to be?"

"Don't start on me, you're the one that insists on doing all the map reading. If you stopped being such a control freak maybe stuff like this wouldn't happen."

"So, you want to be involved, what do you suggest we do now then?" She squared up to him, hands on hips.

The mist swirled around, closing back in, obscuring the lake below. John prised the map out of Suzy's clenched hand and studied it closely. "What about walking down to Harstop instead then taking a cab back to the car?"

"Have you any idea how far that is? At least 50 miles I reckon. They'd have to go all the way up to Penrith before coming all the way back down again. It would cost a flipping fortune."

"Do you have your phone on you?"

"Oh no. I'm not calling Mountain Rescue, not for this. We know where we are and we're not injured. I'm not ruining someone's Saturday night just because you couldn't be arsed to put my head-torch back where it should have been. Anyway, where's your headtorch?"

"Batteries went. I've been meaning to put some new ones in for a while now." John at least had the decency to look sheepish. "I wasn't thinking of calling Mountain Rescue, but we could use the torch on it. How much power do you have?"

Suzy took her phone out of the inside pocket of her waterproof jacket and checked it. "43%. Not much really but it'll have to do."

"Right, well I suggest we crack on. It looks like there's a path down off the end of the crag, let's aim for that and see how far we can get in an hour." He picked up the backpack and helped her slip it back on her shoulders. It was barely in place before she set off at an alarming rate. "It's still quite a way, maybe we need to pace ourselves?" He called, scampering after her.

"You pace yourself, I'm getting out of here as fast as I can." And with that she disappeared off into the mist.

"Oi! Wait for me. We should keep each other in sight at all times in this weather."

"Well you'd better hurry up then, hadn't you?"

At the end of the crag an indistinct and underused path wound down through scree, rocky outcrops and bogs. John picked his way down carefully while Suzy, now a woman on a mission, careered down, slipping over several times; swearing loudly each time. It didn't take long to drop down below the mist and although the path wasn't clear the footbridge was, so at least they had something to aim for. When they reached it Suzy removed her backpack again.

"Now what?" asked John.

"Now we need to get some food and drink into us before we crack on. It'll be dark by the time we reach the top and the rain is coming in so we won't want to stop again." She handed John a flask of tea. "We're going to be walking in the dark now anyway, ten minutes won't make a fat lot of difference either way so let's at least eat something."

John pulled a face as he slurped the tea. "Urrgh! Cold!" He handed it back, removed his own backpack and took a drink from his flask. "Ahhh, that's better. Snickers?"

As they stood on the footbridge eating chocolate the rain began to fall steadily.

"Why do we do this?" He asked "We could be home in front of the fire right now with beer and pizza."

"I know," smiled Suzy, nudging him. "But then we wouldn't have any great stories to tell now, would we? Are you done?"

"Done."

"Right, let's get everything tightly packed so there's no more faffing. I'll keep the map and compass out and you hang onto the torch." She pulled the drawstring tight on the top of her rucksack before swinging it up onto her back. "Ready?"

"Let's do this!"

The disaster was turning into a bit of an adventure and they both set off with a determined spring in their step. The path was steep but easy to follow; they gained height quickly and were soon swallowed up by the mist again.

"Let's take a compass reading," insisted Suzy.

"What, again?"

"Yes, again."

"But you only did one five minutes ago."

"I know, but it's almost dark now and I do NOT want to get lost again, now bring the torch over." John shone the torch on the map and waited while Suzy took a reading. "You really should learn how to do this you know." She muttered as she studied the contours. "According to this our path heads off in that direction but it's so hard to tell."

John shone the torch in the direction she was pointing. "Well, I think I can sort of see a path. Keep the map handy and we'll see where it leads."

They followed the grassy track for fifty metres or so to a junction with a clear stone track. Suzy looked at the map again. "That must mean we're here." She said, pointing to a cross-roads. "This track should lead around past some cairns then off down Kidsty Pike. We'll walk for another couple of minutes then I'll take another reading just to be certain. She turned to set off.

"What the hell is that?" John was shining the torch away into the mist where several pairs of glowing eyes were staring back at them. "It's like the ghosts in Scooby Doo! What the hell are they? They're too tall for sheep."

As they stared the shapes around the eyes slowly emerged until they could make out a small herd of red deer with a magnificent stag in the middle.

"Oh my god!" Breathed Suzy "They are fantastic! Shame our cameras won't work in this light."

Despite the darkness and steady rainfall they both remained stock still and silent as they watched the deer. After a few moments the herd wandered off leaving John and Suzy alone again on the fell.

"See?" Said Suzy "It was worth getting lost just for that!"

"C'mon, we'll never get home at this rate." John took off into the mist with Suzy in hot pursuit. They made quite a pair with Suzy insisting they stop every few minutes to take another map reading and John twisting and turning to make sure there was enough light for them both to see where they were stepping.

Eventually the path began to descend more steeply. "This is good." Smiled Suzy "Assuming we're on the right path, and I'm pretty sure we are, we should hit Kidsty Howes very soon.

"Shit!" John slipped over and fell to earth with a thump.

"Are you OK?"

"Yes. Fine. Just banged my leg. Are my waterproofs OK? I've not ripped them have I?"

"It's well past seven, we're lost on a fell in freezing cold thick mist and rain and you're worried that you might have ripped your waterproof trousers? The fashion police are not out in force tonight you know." Suzy peered at his backside. "No, they look fine. Can we go home now?"

John continued on in sulky silence as they made their way downhill. They soon reached the crags at Kidsty Howes.

"Oh thank god for that – look!" Suzy was pointing down through the thinning mist.

"Haweswater!"

"Better than that, see those lights over there? That's the Haweswater Hotel, so we are definitely on the right path, as long as we take it steady and keep going downhill we'll reach the lake shore, and then all we have to do is turn right and follow the edge of the lake back to the car."

They continued downhill, quicker now they didn't need to stop and check the map every few minutes.

"Did you know there's an old Corpse Road over there?" John shone his torch in the direction of the far side of the lake when they'd paused for a moment.

"Really?"

"Yup. There's a village hidden under the water in the reservoir and before they had a proper church they used to send their dead over the fell to Shap."

"You're not about to start telling me a ghost story are you?"

"No. Although there was one story about..."

"Stop it! Tell me when we're back home with the lights on and a hot dinner in front of us." Suzy turned to carry on. "What was that?"

Several pairs of illuminated green eyes appeared out of the mist.

"Just sheep," smiled John. "Probably wandering what the hell we're doing out here at this time of night. Herdies I think. Did you know they eat their own fleeces if they get buried in the snow?"

"You are a mine of useless information aren't you?"

"You'll thank me for that one day when you're on 'Who Wants to be a Millionaire?'"

They continued making their way downhill until they reached

the main path around the lake.

“Oh thank god for that,” sighed John.

“We’re not done yet, it’s another good mile or so back to the car.”

“Yes, but at least we know where we’re going now, this is the easy part.”

At that precise moment the battery in the phone finally died leaving them stranded in pitch blackness.

“You were saying?”

“Bollocks.”

“We’ll just have to walk really slowly. I’m sure our eyes will get used to the dark. Lucky it’s a rocky path so at least we can see the stones.”

As they picked, slipped and tripped their way along the shore path Suzy paused and pointed over towards the carpark. “Are those lights in the carpark?”

“I think so, yes.”

“What if it’s doggers?”

“What?”

"What if it's doggers? I read about them. What if this place is the hottest dogging spot in Cumbria?"

"Don't be ridiculous!"

"Well, it might be. What do we do then?"

"Head down, eyes front and if anyone invites you into their car, just say no. I don't care how warm and dry it looks!"

They giggled as they made their way along the last few hundred metres to the car park.

"Oh, it's just a campervan," said Suzy as she closed the final gate behind them.

"You sound disappointed."

"Well, it would have livened things up a bit, wouldn't it? What's wrong now?"

"The car keys..."

"Don't even THINK about it! You put them in your inside jacket pocket. I saw you. Now stop winding me up, I'm flipping freezing."

John grinned, fished out the keys and opened the driver's door.

"Pop the boot door for me," called Suzy "I want to dump all my wet stuff in there – no point soaking the back seat."

The rear door of the car swung open and she quickly dropped her wet coat and leggings inside. As she was about to close it, something in the door pocket caught her eye, she picked it up, slammed the door and quickly jumped into the passenger seat.

"I've put your seat heater on and cranked the heating to max." John turned to look at her as she stared at him stonily. "What?"

She held out her hand, opening it slowly. A flash of recognition crossed John's face. "Oooohhh... so that's where I put it." He grinned, looking at the headtorch in her hand.

"Good job I flipping love you!" said Suzy, leaning back in her seat.

"Now I suggest you drive home quickly, before I put this somewhere we'll both regret."

HAWESWATER – IN REAL LIFE

Haweswater Reservoir was created in the 1930s to provide drinking water for Manchester. Prior to that there was a much smaller lake and two villages: Mardale Green near what is now the car park and Measland further along the valley. The village of Burnbanks at the north end of the valley was created to house the dam workers and was only ever intended to be a temporary structure; however it still stands and makes a lovely stopping off point on a walk around the lake.

Before there was any consecrated ground in Mardale Green the villagers had to carry their dead over the fell to Shap. From the mid 1700s they were able to bury them in the tiny churchyard in the village but, when the dam project was announced, all of the remains were moved to Shap. The final service was held in Mardale church on 18 August 1935 where the Bishop of Carlisle spoke to over 1000 people gathered in the church and around the nearby fields.

A golden eagle used to live in crags around Riggindale Valley, near where the story takes place, but he sadly disappeared a few years ago. We all live in hope that the eagles will one day return to the valley.

CHANCE ENCOUNTER

"Do you need a hand?"

Angela squinted up into the sunshine from her seat on the kerb. The voice came from a woman with short blonde hair who looked to be about her own age. She smiled as she crouched down and repeated the question. "Do you need a hand? I've changed plenty of wheels in my time."

"Yes, please – I know I should know how to do this but I've never had to do it in real life before. I'm trying to undo the nuts but the wheel keeps spinning around."

"That's because you need to loosen them before you jack it up. I'm Sarah by the way." Sarah jumped up, smoothed down her jeans and walked over to the boot of her car. She returned a moment or two later with an impressive looking toolkit. "Ex army mechanic." She said in response to Angela's quizzical look. "I spent 20 years fixing cars, tanks and whatever else needed fixing, all over the world. I don't feel dressed without my toolkit." She released the jack, dropping the car back onto the road.

"I'm Angela. Will you teach me how to do it? I don't want to be a useless woman; I want to learn how to fix things. I've always been fascinated with how stuff works."

"No problem, first of all you'll need one of these." Sarah produced a wheel wrench and deftly extended it. "The longer it is the easier it will be to undo the nuts." She set to work with Angela watching her closely. "So, what are you doing in Wreay?"

"Long story, but the short version is that I'm here to look around the church." She gestured to the ornate building behind her, its basilican features at odds with the rest of the cottages clustered around the village green . "I'm fascinated by Sarah Losh. You?"

"Short story, I came for a hike, a pub lunch and a look around the church. I only live in Penrith but I'd never heard of Sarah Losh until I read a piece about her in Cumbria Life. I don't get the magazine, I flicked through it in the waiting room at the dentist last week. Sorry, can I just move around there?"

Angela scootched along the kerb giving Sarah a bit more space and peered into the toolkit. "Is it OK for me to have a rummage?"

"Yes, of course, go ahead. So, what do you know about Sarah Losh then?"

"Well, I'm not an expert but I know that she was a remarkable woman and very well educated for her time. She kept pushing back the boundaries in an era when women were supposed to 'know their place'." Angela picked up a number of items and examined each one before putting it back. "I love that when she redesigned the church she chose to use local people so she could support the community and I really admire that about her. What's this for?"

"It's a clamp, you never know when you might need one and always worth keeping a couple handy. Right, that's all the nuts loosened, do you want to jack it up again now?" Sarah wiped her hands on a cloth as Angela put the jack back into place and began winding the handle to extend it. "This is a pretty fancy car; doesn't it come with some sort of breakdown recovery?"

"Yes, there's a button next to the rear view mirror that I can push to summon help, but it's only a flat tyre and I want to be more self sufficient. I'm fed up with having people run around doing things for me."

Sarah watched as Angela struggled to jack up the car. "Need a hand?"

"No – I want to do this myself."

As she was kneeling down Sarah noticed the discrete Jimmy Choo badge on Angela's shoes; not the big logo splashed across his cheaper high street range but the understated tag for those who didn't want, or need, to show off. Her Gucci jeans and jacket were immaculate as were her nails and smartly bobbed hair and on the soft cream leather passenger seat of the car sat a large Fendi handbag.

"There," breathed Angela. "Is that high enough?"

Sarah crouched down to check the height "Yes, that should do it. Do you want to finish removing the nuts or shall I?"

"I'll have a go, pass me the spanner thingy."

"It's a wrench." Sarah passed it over and Angela immediately got to work.

"You say 'ex army mechanic', why did you leave, if you don't mind me asking?" Angela began working her way around the nuts.

"Not at all. I got fed up of the travel and not having anywhere to call home. It was great at first, and I really have seen the world, but I just want to stay in one place, be part of a community and not worry that I'm about to get dropped into another war zone."

"Can you hold these for me?" Angela passed over the nuts as she removed them from the wheel. "I completely understand, well, not the war zone part, but I've had to travel a lot with my job and, to be honest, I began to crave a cosy night in front of the fire with only the cats and some trashy TV for company."

"What did you do?"

"I was an actress, I starred in a couple of big movies, most people have usually recognised me by now. I'm rather glad you haven't." She looked up and smiled at Sarah.

"Sorry, I've been out of the country a lot and I'm don't watch many films, I generally prefer the books."

"Me too, to be honest. I'm not really sure how it all happened. A talent scout spotted me in a show we did at the end of my drama degree and next thing you know I'm snogging Ben Affleck in the back of a car in 'Racing Moonshine'"

"I thought that was Judy Wreay? Oh wait, that's you isn't it? And that's why you're in Wreay village?"

"Yes, and sort of. My real name is Angela Wigglesworth but that wasn't starry enough so I took the name Judy from Judy Garland

and Wreay as it's where my mum grew up. There, that's all the nuts off, now what?"

"Now we need to get the wheel off, help me give it a wiggle." With one each side of the wheel they wiggled it until it dropped to the floor. "Where's your spare?"

"In the boot, it was a bit heavy to lift out."

"No worries, I'll have it out in a jiffy."

Sarah disappeared into the boot and with a few grunts had the spare wheel out on the pavement. She rolled it along to where Angela was sitting. "My turn to ask." she said smiling "Why did you leave?"

"A very good question!" Angela sat cross-legged on the pavement for a while and paused as she searched for the right words. "In a nutshell I was fed up of fake. What you see is never what you get and real friends are hard to find." Her gaze fell to her hands and she twiddled the rings on her right hand absentmindedly as she continued. "Chaotic filming schedules meant I lost contact with most of my friends from uni and, once you're famous, it's hard to know if someone's with you because they want to be with you or just because of who you are. All the guessing wore me out."

Sarah rolled the spare wheel to the empty space on the front of the car. "This is only a space saver so no speeding and you'll have to get the proper one back on as soon as possible. The friends thing must be frustrating." She paused, squinting as the sun reflected from the car window into her eyes. "I had the opposite problem but the same result; army life meant we were thrown together with people, so much so that we were more like family than friends, but then I worked in war zones and some of those friends got killed, so I kind of drew back and started keeping myself to myself."

"I'm so sorry to hear that, and actually that's another reason I escaped. I was fed up with this idea that we were doing something amazing when all we were doing was acting and getting paid a lot of money for it." She paused for a moment, staring at the floor and allowed her hair to hide her face as a chattering group of people passed them on the pavement. As they disappeared around the corner she looked back up. "I could see that it was all fake but so many people really believed it. I knew there were people like you out there doing real work but not getting recognised and certainly not getting paid what we were."

"I can't imagine that being recognised is all it's cracked up to be. Right, this is the tricky part, we need to lift the wheel onto the studs and it all has to be aligned or it won't go on. Let me have a go on my own first and if I fail miserably you can join in."

Angela shifted around so she was out of Sarah's way but could still see what she was doing. "You're right, getting recognised is no fun. Well, it was at first, but then it just got to be a real pain. I always had to look perfect, even when I was just going to the shops, or for a walk in the woods; there'd always be someone with a phone ready to take a snap of me not looking my best." She studied her reflection in the bodywork for a moment. "I couldn't even go out for pizza in peace – do you know that one time someone just pulled a chair up to the table where I was eating with my agent and thought they could just join in?"

"Seriously? That is so rude! Right, are you ready? How does this look?"

Angela got onto her hands and knees and peered along the line of the wheel. "Looks about right I think."

"1,2,3 and uuuuupppp she goes." Sarah lifted the wheel and tried hooking it onto the studs but didn't quite manage it and the wheel dropped to the floor again. "Damn. Sometimes they go on sweet as a nut and sometimes I swear they're possessed by the devil himself!" She stood on the kerb stretching her back. "Another reason for leaving – too much heavy lifting didn't do my back any good either."

"Let me buy you lunch when we're finished – it's the least I can do, and the pub over there looks nice enough."

"Deal. Oh wait, I've had an idea." Sarah rummaged around in her tool bag. "Aha! Thought I had one of these in here!" She produced a long cylindrical piece of metal.

"What on earth is that?"

"It's a wheel alignment guide." Said Sarah gleefully, "And it's going to save us loads of time!" She deftly attached the guide to the wheel stud and in less than 30 seconds had the wheel aligned and back on the car. "Right, all we need to do now is put all the nuts back on, tighten them all up and you're done. Here you go." She handed the nuts to Angela. "So, what's next for you?"

"Dunno really." Angela paused for a moment as she began trying to tighten the nut.

"Not too tight, literally just wind them on with your fingers and we'll tighten them afterwards when the car is back on the ground."

"Oh, OK. It's hard really as acting is all I know, and I'm lucky enough to have made enough money from it that I never need to work again, but I can't imagine sitting around for the rest of my life with nothing to do. I was thinking I might volunteer somewhere, but I don't know what or where yet. What about you?"

"Similar story, army disability pension means I don't need to work but I definitely need something to do – I was hoping Sarah Losh might inspire me."

"You plan to design churches?" laughed Angela.

"Not quite, but I need to do something with my hands. Is that all of the nuts back on?"

"Yes, do I lower the jack now?" Sarah nodded and Angela started winding the jack and lowering the car back down to the ground. "The thing is, even with all the attention I still feel like a fraud inside; the only thing I could do was act a bit and now I've packed that it I'm a bit lost to be honest. All my old friends are well settled into their careers with husbands and families and here I am, a washed up single 40 something who lives alone with her cats and can't even change a wheel on her car!"

"Well I can't argue with the rest of it, but you definitely know how to change a wheel now. If you learned that today just think what you could learn tomorrow. Here," Sarah handed over the wrench "tighten them up in this order." She pointed to the nuts one at a time and Angela obligingly tightened them. "Once they're all done then we get to jump on the wrench just to make sure."

"Maybe I could go back to school, Open University or something like that?"

"And study what?"

"Car mechanics?"

"Seriously?"

"No, just kidding. I've always been fascinated with psychology and helping people so perhaps I'll give that a go."

"Sounds like a great idea, right now for the fun part, just watch your Jimmy Choos!"

Angela laughed as Sarah pushed the wrench onto one of the nuts, steadied herself on the car and stepped up onto the handle jigging up and down to tighten it.

"They're supposed to be properly torqued," she said. "I don't have the right tool for that, but this'll do for now. Your turn."

They both giggled as they took turns jumping up and down on the wrench tightened the nuts one by one.

"There we go, all done." Sarah wiped the wrench, put it back with the other tools and zipped the bag up. "I'll pop this into the car, then how about we wander around the church together? It's been a while since I had a fun afternoon and a good old natter."

Anglea leaned against the car and smiled. "That sounds absolutely perfect."

WREAY – IN REAL LIFE

Wreay is a pretty little village just south of Carlisle and very near to the M6 motorway. There are some excellent short walks in the area and the village boasts its own flag, one version of which was flown at the South Pole and can be viewed in the village pub.

Sarah Losh was a 19th century architect and designer, she was very well educated for a woman of that time and also well travelled. She used her own money to fund her architectural projects in the village, the most notable of which is the village church built in the style of a Basilica, which has been described as one of the most interesting buildings in England.

The Sarah Losh Heritage Centre is a short walk from the village and contains information and artefacts from her life. From there it's an easy walk back to the pub where they serve good beer and excellent food.

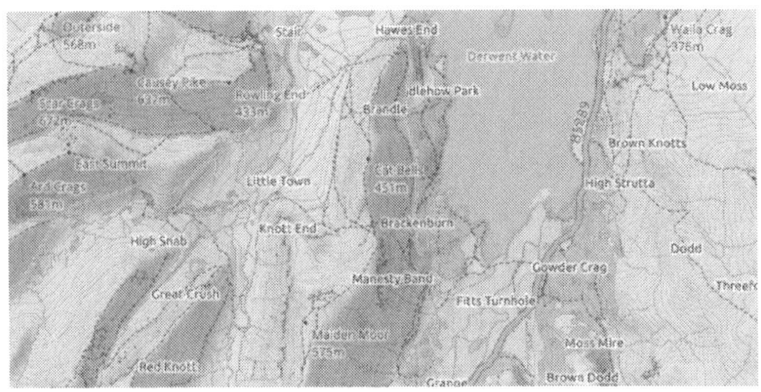

FINDERS KEEPERS

"Are they looking?" hissed Oliver, trying to look nonchalant as he prodded his walking pole around in the pool at the base of the waterfall. Water splashed onto his trendy white trainers and sunlight glinted off his new found treasure in the watery gravel below.

Isaac peered over at their parents, sat on a rock 20 meters or so below them on the hillside. "Nah, they're still drinking tea and trying to get a phone signal by the looks of it. Dad's probably looking for jobs again, it's all he ever does since his office closed. Hope he finds one then we can go back to Florida again instead of being stuck here."

Oliver glanced at his kid brother and grinned. "Come on then, let's see what this is." He held out his arm "Hang on to me while I reach down and grab it."

Isaac hopped across the rocks towards him, pausing to catch his balance a couple of times as his feet slipped on the moss. He landed with a thud next to his brother. "What is it Ollie?" he asked, as they peered into the pool.

"Hard to say, but you hold my arm and I'll fish it out."

Isaac grabbed Ollie's outstretched arm with both hands and leaned back ready to take his weight.

"Ready?"

"Ready"

Ollie reached down, stretching out over the pool towards the shining object, his brother hanging to his other arm with all his might.

"Have you got it? Have you got it?" asked Isaac excitedly.

"Give me a chance!" Ollie pushed his fair hair back out of his eyes before plunging his arm deep into the icy cold water.

"Don't get your shoes wet, mum'll kill you!" squeaked Isaac.

"Got it!" said Ollie "Pull me back in!"

Isaac yanked extra hard on Ollie's arm and they both toppled onto the gravelly grass next to the waterfall. "Watch it!" grunted Ollie, shoving his kid brother off him and rolling away.

Isaac peered over the top of a nearby rock to check on their parents. Red Crag and High Spy loomed large behind them. They'd started out on Cat Bells then followed the route up and over High Spy before dropping down from Dale Head Tarn and had just finished their lunch sitting alongside the waterfall.

Ollie dusted himself down and straightened his hair while Isaac, his black hair pointing in every direction, used the sleeve of his hand-me-down blue hoodie to wipe his nose. He then used his other sleeve to clean the dirt off his face but only succeeded in smearing it from one cheek across to the other.

"You're disgusting!"

"Yeah, and you're only trying to look cool in case that girl from the B&B comes past."

Ollie flushed and shoved his little brother. Isaac stumbled a few paces then turned and lunged at him, his head landing squarely in Ollie's stomach.

"Ow!" shouted Ollie as he hit the ground.

"What are you two up to?" shouted dad "You're not fighting again are you?"

"No, I just slipped on a rock," answered Ollie, glaring as Isaac "Pack it in," he hissed "or they'll come up here and want to know what this is." He opened his hand to reveal what looked like a battered old bangle.

"Sorry"

They both peered over the rock and smiled and waved at their parents.

"You want some cake?" asked mum

"No, we're good thanks!" shouted Isaac, ignoring his mother's surprised look and turning back to Ollie. "What do you think it is?"

"Dunno"

They both looked closely at the object. It appeared to be an old silver bangle with some indistinct writing around the inside. The catch was broken and it looked as if there was a stone missing from the front.

"Should we tell mum and dad?" asked Isaac.

"Why on earth would we do that?" scoffed Ollie "They'd only take it off us. Finders keepers is my motto!"

"What does the writing say?"

Ollie turned the bangle in his hand, screwing up his eyes and twisting his body towards the sunshine to get a better look at it. Part of it was shiny from being in the water but other bits of the writing were obscured by mud. "I'll run it under the waterfall to try and clean it up a bit."

He stepped up to the waterfall, straddled two rocks, and leaned one arm on a nearby ledge as he reached his other arm out and let the water run over the bangle in his outstretched hand. As he turned it a couple of times there was a deep rumble from behind the waterfall and the ground beneath their feet shuddered as if a giant lorry had just driven by. Ollie quickly jumped back.

"What was that?" breathed Isaac, his eyes wide with fear and excitement.

"Absolutely no idea." replied Ollie, studying the waterfall to see where the noise had come from, but everything looked perfectly normal. He turned the bangle in his hand using his thumbnail to scratch away some of the mud. "I think it's Roman numerals." He said, leaning over to show Isaac. "We did them in school last term."

Isaac looked at the faint lines of C's, X's and I's "So?"

"So maybe it's a Roman bangle and maybe there are more like it nearby."

"Oooohhh. Try running it under the water again to clear off the rest of the mud."

Ollie resumed his position next to the waterfall and, as he placed his hand back on the ledge, the rumbling began again. He pulled his hand away sharply and the rumbling stopped.

Isaac jumped up and down with excitement "It's when you put your hand on that spot – do it again!"

Ollie adjusted his position and put his hand back on the ledge. Nothing. He looked puzzled.

"You moved your feet," said Isaac "Put them back where they were and do it again."

Ollie carefully put his feet exactly where they had previously been and placed his hand back on the ledge. The rumbling began again."

Isaac dropped to his hands and knees to peer behind the water. "The rock's moving! There's a cave behind!" he shouted excitedly.

"Ssshhhhh – keep it down!"

"Sorry"

The rumbling stopped and they both squeezed behind the waterfall and into the cool darkness of the cave beyond. Ollie reached into his jacket pocket, took his phone out and used his torch app to light up the room.

"When did mum give you your phone back?" asked Isaac

"She didn't, I just took it out of her bag when she wasn't looking. It's my phone so it's not stealing."

As he swung the beam around the cave it illuminated the dank, musty interior. It was the size of a small church hall with boulders around the edges and a series of busts with inscriptions underneath them.

"Boring!" grumbled Isaac "I thought at least there'd be a skeleton or loads of gold or something."

Ollie scanned his torch along the far wall "Look!" He said "An alter!"

They crept along the cave, eyes fixed on the alter at the far end. In a recess, just above it, was another statue but this time it was a whole person, not just a bust. It stood about 2 feet high and was made of smooth red marble. Around it were scattered coins and what looked like the remains of other bangles and jewellery, all tarnished and rusty thanks to the dampmess of the cave.

"I think this might be a secret temple," said Ollie, his voice unnaturally hushed. "Mr Peacock told us about them."

"So who's that then?" asked Isaac, pointing at the statue.

"One of their gods probably. Might even be Saturn – I think he was the most important. They used to make statues of them and then leave money and jewellery next to them to get on their good side."

"Swot!" teased Isaac. "There's hundreds of coins here, won't they be worth something? What should we do with them?"

"Grab what you can. Stuff your pockets and say nothing to no-one," instructed Ollie propping his torch on the alter so they could see what they were doing.

"What will we do with them?"

"Stop asking so many questions and start stuffing – mum and dad will be after us soon."

Both boys started crawling around the dusty cave floor, grabbing what they could and stuffing them into all the available pockets on their trousers and jackets. Ollie was now less concerned about his trendy white trainers and more concerned about grabbing as many coins as he could. "When we get home I'll talk to Carl Standring, I bet his big brother will buy them off us. Might even get enough for a new skateboard or even an Xbox."

"What about me?" asked Isaac

"Yeah, well, if there's any money left over we'll get you something too. Is that all of them?" Ollie swung his torch around one last time.

"Looks like it."

"Right, dust yourself down and remember, not a word to mum and dad!"

"OK," said Isaac, squinting as he followed his big brother back out into the warm sunshine.

"You two have been quiet, what have you been up to?" asked mum as they trotted back down the hill towards them.

"Oh, nothing much," smiled Isaac. "Ollie has just been telling me all about the Roman Empire."

The ground finished rumbling beneath their feet.

"Did you feel that?" asked mum. "That's the fourth time that's happened. What on earth could it be?"

Ollie and Isaac exchanged a quick glance. "Probably rockfalls – last one back to the B&B stinks like a pig!" shouted Ollie as he and Isaac raced ahead of their parents down the path, their pockets heavy with their new-found wealth.

CATBELLS – IN REAL LIFE

Catbells is one of the most popular fells in the Lake District, being within striking distance of Keswick. It's a straightforward climb and great for families as the large flat(ish) ridge leading towards the summit offers spectacular views of the surrounding fells and there's a pleasing scramble to trig point at the top.

Adventurous folks can then continue their route, as the family in the story did, along to Maiden Moor and High Spy before dropping back down along Newlands Beck. There are a number of interesting waterfalls along the way, although I can't promise you'll find hidden treasure behind any of them...

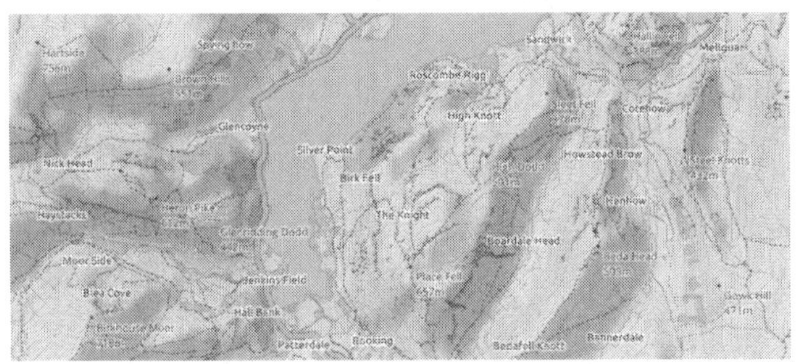

ROUND THE BEND

Alan was an optimist. "I'm sure it will be brighter next week." He'd say, in the middle of the worst summer on record.

Cycling was his thing. His garage was full of bikes, bits of bikes and bits which may, or may not, once have been part of a bike. There was a "sort of" filing system; his intentions had been good when he started out but now all the things that were in neatly labelled tins and tubs were outnumbered, and largely hidden, by the things that weren't.

Alan looked out of his bedroom window into the thick mist outside.

"It'll brighten up by lunchtime." He muttered, pulling on his cycling shorts and top. Eddy, his tortoiseshell cat, peered up at him suspiciously and shifted her position on the bed. Although a female cat Eddy was named after one of his cycling heroes, Eddy

Merckx; Alan thought it suited her perfectly.

He straightened the bed around her and walked through to the kitchen to make breakfast.

His Kendal flat was basic and tiny, but tiny meant no mortgage. After his mother died he invested most of the money she left him into the flat and had been living off the rest. He'd been lucky to find a place with its own garage, even if it was in a communal block at the end of the cul-de-sac. Sadly, funds were now beginning to dwindle and Alan needed to find some work.

He reached a tin of cat food from the cupboard and Eddy magically appeared at his feet. "Sorry it's not the posh pouches anymore," he said, in response to Eddy's disapproving look. "Tins are cheap so you'll just have to get used to them I'm afraid." As he put the food down he paused to pick up the old bits of cat food scattered across the floor. "Of course it would save me a fortune if you could just eat your food, rather than scattering around the kitchen," he teased as he tickled her behind the ears. She ignored him and continued eating.

The boiling kettle clicked and Alan breathed deep, inhaling the aroma of hot coffee as he poured the boiling water onto the instant granules. Reaching the milk from the fridge he splashed some into his mug and poured the rest onto his cereal before popping the now empty container onto the burgeoning recycling pile. He wandered into the lounge and perched at his tiny dining table as he leafed through the local paper.

"New Plans for Old Landmark"

"Local Car Park Closed for Refurbishment"

"Kendal Courier Sheepish after Accident"

The final story was about a local parcel delivery firm who'd missed an important delivery after the driver had sped around a bend and collided with a hapless sheep in the middle of the road.

"Wouldn't have happened if he'd been on a bike," muttered Alan, idly stirring his coffee. As he looked at the photo of the van he had an idea and, without moving his eyes from the newspaper, put his spoon down directly onto the table, just to the left of the place mat. Then he shifted his gaze to the window and finally to Eddy who was, by now, examining the sofa to select the perfect sleeping position for the day.

"What this place needs is a cycle courier," he announced. Eddy looked unimpressed.

Leaving his half eaten cereal going soggy in the bowl he flipped open his laptop and began searching the internet to see if it had already been done. It hadn't. Alan had found his niche.

"Cumbria Cycle Couriers – Geared for Success"

At lunchtime he was still sat in his cycling shorts, cold coffee and long forgotten soggy cereal beside him. He'd got a lot done though; he'd bagged the name on Facebook, Twitter and Instagram, registered the website address and had even begun developing a logo.

He stood up, stretched his aching limbs and wandered over to the window. The sunshine reflected from the windows of the apartments opposite made him squint "I told you it would brighten up," he said to Eddy, now fast asleep and long past caring.

Alan ran a comb through his salt and pepper hair, grabbed his cycle helmet and headed downstairs.

"Good morning!" He shouted to his neighbour Mrs Sharp as he locked the garage behind him and wheeled his bike out onto the lane.

Alan cycled into town and, after carefully chaining his bike to a nearby lamppost, he wandered in to his favourite local coffee shop where his good friend Jenna worked.

"Morning!" he called as he barrelled through the door, almost colliding with another customer on their way out.

"Afternoon." Jenna smiled back. "You're running late today."

"I've had a busy morning!" he beamed before filling her in on his brilliant new plan while she made his coffee.

"Int it a bit 'illy for a cycle courier around here?" asked Jenna, cleaning the nozzle on the milk steamer before handing Alan his coffee.

"Not a problem if you're used to it. I cycle around here all the time, loads of people do – hey, maybe I could even recruit some of the guys from the cycle club?"

Alan's enthusiasm began seeping in to Jenna. "Do you really think you could make it work?" she asked, leaning on the counter.

"Don't see why not – nothing ventured, nothing gained and all that!"

"Excuse me," a voice piped up. "I couldn't help overhearing your conversation."

Alan and Jenna turned, following the voice to a smartly dressed man at a nearby table. His iPad was open at a "very important email" and a half finished latte sat next to him alongside a yet to be started goats cheese ciabatta.

“My name’s Doug,” he continued. "I was supposed to be popping over to Glenridding after lunch to drop off some important documents at the hotel there, but the wife’s just sent me a text saying that she’s working late so I need to pick up the kids from school in Lancaster. I’m willing to give you £20 to take this envelope over to Glenridding for me.” He produced a fat, brown A4 envelope from the man-bag at his feet. “I’ve seen you in here a few times so I trust you – your first fare, whaddya say?”

Alan grinned triumphantly “I say yes!” and he thrust out his hand. Doug gave him the envelope then reached into his wallet and handed over a £20 note.

“Just hand it in to reception at the Glenridding Hotel, it’s for the manager and he’s expecting it.” As he said this he pulled a business card from his pocket and handed it to Alan. “Call me if there are any problems.” Then he turned to Jenna, handing her the ciabattia. “Could you wrap this for me to go please?”

“Thank you, thank you, thank you, I promise I won’t let you down.” chattered Alan excitedly. “Here’s my mobile number too, just in case.” He scrawled his number on the corner of a napkin and handed it over.

“Like I said, I trust you, and admire your enthusiasm.” Doug gulped down the last of his coffee, grabbed his sandwich from Jenna and raced out of the door.

Alan hopped excitedly from foot to foot, clutching the envelope with both hands, his eyes gleaming with excitement.

Jenna looked at her watch "It's a fair way to Glenridding and back, are you sure you can do it?"

"Of course, done it loads of times – it's June so it won't be dark for ages yet. My first customer on day one – I *knew* this was a great idea!"

Alan gulped down his coffee, blowing into it impatiently in an effort to cool it down. He hovered around the counter forcing a chuckling Jenna to dodge around him as she served the other customers.

"Right, I'm off!" he announced. Jenna handed him his freshly filled water bottle and he slipped the envelope into his rucksack before racing out of the door. Two minutes later he returned. "Forgot my cycle helmet," he grinned, grabbing it from the counter. "See you later!"

Alan unchained his bike and set off out of Kendal like Bradley Wiggins on the last stage of the Tour de France. He was a man on a mission as he powered out of town and up to Plumgarth's roundabout, banking keenly as he zoomed around the roundabout and onto the A591. "Piece of cake," he said to himself, smiling.

As he sped towards Ings the skies darkened and the heavens opened, soaking him to the skin within minutes. He pulled into the petrol station to pick up a couple of Mars bars and a plastic bag to keep the precious envelope dry in his rucksack. Back out on the road he swished, splished and splashed his way towards Windermere and soon he was swinging around the small white traffic island and off up Kirkstone Pass.

Not long after he started the climb, at a point where the road narrows around an old stone house, Alan came across a bus versus motorhome standoff. It was stalemate. Both vehicles were refusing to budge. He wheeled his bike up to the side of the motorhome and propped it against a nearby wall.

"Why should I have to move?" shouted the driver when Alan approached him. "He could see me coming and put his foot down on purpose!"

Alan plodded through the rain to the bus driver. "Blooming tourists! Bane of my chuffing life!" he ranted. "Takes me twice as flipping long to get anywhere this time of year. It's my last run of the day too!"

"Couldn't you just back up a little bit and maybe pull your wing mirrors in?" Alan suggested.

"No!"

Alan peered along the bus at half a dozen or so fed up looking faces peering through the steamed up windows. "The sooner you can get to Kendal then the sooner you can get home" suggested Alan as rain dripped from his nose.

The driver glared at him. Alan smiled hopefully. Finally, muttering oaths under his breath that Alan was quite glad he couldn't hear the driver slammed the bus into reverse, backed up the bare minimum distance he could and the motorhome squeezed through. "Thank you," smiled Alan, waving at the bus driver, but he ignored him, as did the motorhome driver as they sped past splashing through a puddle and covering Alan in muddy water.

"Well, I was wet already." He peered down at his sodden socks, picked up his bike and carried on up the hill.

Alan huffed and puffed his way up the hill. "What would Eddy do, what would Eddy do, what would Eddy do?" He chanted away under his breath to push himself on. The occasional car raced past him as he slowly made his way up the hill.

As he neared the top of the pass the rain eased to a drizzle and the mist materialised, clinging to fields, walls, hedges and Alan.

Rounding a bend he came face to face with a Herdwick ewe and her fuzzy felt black lamb, slap bang in the middle of the road.

"Hello there gorgeous," said Alan, smiling as he came to a halt. "Are you lovely ladies going to let me squeeze past?" The sheep continued looking at him, chewing like sullen teenagers in a Wild West show. "Come on ladies." He said "I'm on a mission and I need to get a very important parcel to Glenridding – I'm only doing this to save you being hit by another lunatic in a white van."

Just then a lunatic in a white van careered around the corner towards them and both sheep took flight. With their back legs nearly catching up with their front they raced to the top of a nearby embankment while the van, which had barely slowed, accelerated away. The sheep continued chewing on the fresh grass as if nothing had happened.

Alan plodded on along the final stretch to the summit, the pass feeling much tougher than usual. "Come on legs," he muttered determinedly. "Not far to the top now then it's all downhill from there." He tried not to think about the journey home.

As he paused for a drink at the picnic tables outside the Kirkstone Inn he gave his bike a quick once over. "Well, that explains it," he said, spotting a flat back tyre. "I thought that were tougher than usual."

He wheeled his bike over into the car park where he had a bit more space and a little bit of shelter behind the dry stone wall. A cool wind had appeared and was whipping up and over the top of the pass, carrying a little of Alan's optimism with it. "Oh well, at least I have all the right kit with me." He sighed as he up-ended his bike and got to work.

Fifteen minutes later he was speeding down towards Brother's Water, the mist was fast disappearing and the breeze was drying him out. "Not far now." He chuckled as he swooped down through the bends on the pass. Suddenly his bike hit a patch of oil, he held on tight and did his best to keep it upright as it veered sharply left then right, but his back wheel caught a rock, forcing his front wheel onto the verge and launched Alan over the handle bars. He torpedoed through a nearby hedge and landed in a sore and sorry heap in the field beyond. He sat there, dazed for a moment.

"You alright mate?" A face peered over the hedge at him. "I was following you down the hill; that was quite a tumble – are you OK?"

Alan looked down at his legs. Everything seemed OK, there was a deep scratch on his right calf and his left arm felt sore and bruised from his landing, but nothing was broken. "I think I'm OK, thank yo." He tried to smile back. His body was fine but his pride had taken a beating. "Is my bike ok?"

"Yes, looks fine," his Good Samaritan replied. "I picked it up out of the road and propped it against the hedge."

Alan pulled himself to his feet with a deep sigh. Today was really not going according to plan! "I'll be there in a mo!" he shouted to his rescuer as he made his way along the hedge to a gate. It was locked. He muttered oaths to himself as he clambered gingerly over.

"Here you go – are you sure you're OK?" the stranger asked as Alan checked over his bike. "That looks like a nasty scratch on your leg."

"I'll be fine; thank you." Alan replied "I'm only going to Glenridding, so I'm nearly there." He dug into his rucksack, found his spare T-shirt and tied it around his now bleeding leg. "That'll do until I can sort it out later."

"I'm Craig. I'd offer you a lift but I've only got a small sport car so nowhere for your bike I'm afraid."

"No, really, I'll be fine." insisted Alan, forcing a smile. "Honestly, I really appreciate your help, but it's only a few minutes from here and then I can get properly cleaned up."

"Well, if you're certain..."

"Yes, absolutely, thank you." he said, his determination resurfacing. "I promise I'll be OK."

"Well, alright then, if you're sure." replied Craig "You take care now." He smiled as he jumped into his car and took off up the hill.

A battered, bruised and somewhat less perkier than usual Alan sighed, mounted his bike and carefully cycled the last mile or so to Glenridding. When he arrived at the hotel he wiped his feet on the mat and handed the envelope to the guy on reception.

"I have a package here for the manager." said Alan, with a weak smile. "I believe he's expecting it."

“I’m the manager.” said a voice behind him. “And you look like you’ve been in the wars.”

“Yeah, it’s been an interesting journey,” replied Alan, turning around. He filled the manager in on the events of the day. When he finished his story the manager smiled.

"Look, I tell you what, you go and have a drink in the bar, on me. I need to sort out a couple of bits and pieces and then I can give you a lift to Penrith station if that will help? I’m heading over there for a meeting and you can get a train back to Oxenholme.”

“Oh, that would be very kind of you – are you sure it’s not trouble?”

“Not at all, I have a Land Rover so the bike will fit in easily.” the manager replied. “John.” He said, addressing the guy behind the reception desk. “See that Alan here gets a drink and a pizza in the bar.” John smiled and nodded. The manager turned to Alan “I’ll see you in half an hour. I’m George, by the way.” He offered his hand.

“Perfect, thank you George.” said Alan taking his hand and shaking it gratefully.

Alan tidied himself up in the gents – the scratch on his leg had stopped bleeding but he had a huge bruise appearing on his arm. Returning to the bar he rapidly devoured his pizza and a pint of bitter shandy before the manager re-appeared. “Sorry,” he said. “Those bits and pieces took a little longer than expected – you good to go now?”

“Yes, thank you so much.” Alan winced as he stood up, his sore limbs now stiffening up.

They quickly loaded the bike into the Land Rover and chatted amiably as they drove to Penrith. “Here you go,” said George as they pulled up outside the station.“Now, are you sure you’ll be OK from here?”

“Yes, absolutely.” replied Alan “I can’t thank you enough for this.”

"It's no problem at all." smiled George. "Now you take care – and good luck with your business venture." With that he pulled away.

Alan wheeled his bike into the ticket office. "Can I have a single to Oxenholme please?" He asked when he reached the window.

"You taking your bike with you?"

"Yes"

"Sorry sir, all bikes need to be pre-booked on to Virgin Trains and I'm afraid the next train, and the one after that, are fully booked."

Alan's heart sank. As he stared at the ticket office clerk he could hear his heart beating in his ears as he digested what he had just heard. "But, it's only one bike and only one stop," ventured Alan.

"Sorry sir, those are the rules, all bikes must be pre-booked."

Alan was crestfallen. "Oh, well, thank you anyway." He wheeled his bike back out into the car park where he stood for a moment, staring at the remains of the castle opposite, then gazing around the car park blankly. He was cold, he was tired, he was sore and, to be honest, he was a little bit fed up. He leaned against the wall of the station for a few moments, resting his head against the large sandstone bricks. A catalogue of other failed ventures raced through his mind. All he needed was a lucky break. Just one. He didn't want to make millions, just take care of himself and his cat. Was that too much to ask? After a few moments he took a very deep breath, "Right." He said out loud, not noticing that he'd startled a nearby couple. "It's no good moping around. What would Eddy do?"

He grabbed his bike firmly by the handlebars and began to wheel it out towards the road. "At least it's mostly downhill from here." He swung his leg over, clicked his feet into place on the pedals and headed for home.

KIRKSTONE PASS – IN REAL LIFE

Kirkstone Pass reaches a height of 454m and is one of the most popular road passes in the Lake District. It takes its name from a stone at the top of the pass which resembles a church steeple – 'kirk' comes from the ancient Norse for 'church'.

The beautiful green Kirkstone Slate is still quarried in the area. In the past, lead and copper was also mined locally and the entrances to some of the mine shafts are still evident in the surrounding hills.

Kirkstone Pass Inn at the top of the pass is one of the highest inns in England. The large carpark opposite is the perfect place to pause for a photograph or a hike up nearby Red Scree. It's also a good place for spotting inversions in the spring and autumn when mist fills the valleys leaving clear blue skies above.

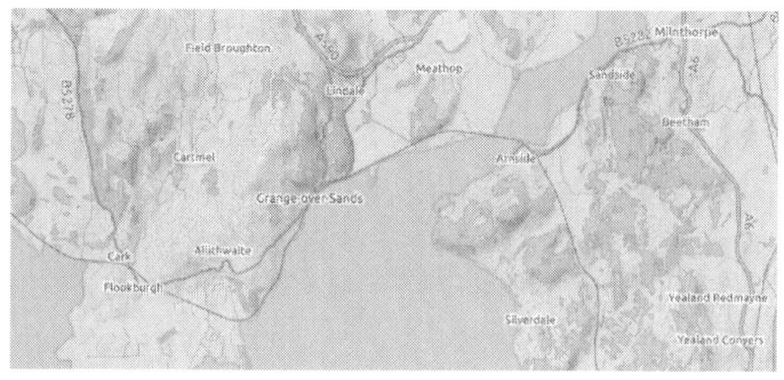

STONE COLD CALLER

Alexa twisted the rear-view mirror so she could see herself. She ran a finger around the edge of her lips to remove tiny smudges of scarlet lipstick; she plucked two stray hairs from the collar of her ink black jacket and checked that the rest of her short dark hair was still precisely in place.

Satisfied she returned the mirror to its original position and looked around outside. Grange-over-Sands, retirees paradise. She surveyed the line of smart bungalows with lawns as neatly manicured as her nails. She'd been watching the street for a few weeks now and was familiar with the comings and goings of each one. The car door creaked as she opened it and swung her legs out, shiny black heels clicking on the pavement; deep breath, big smile. She walked up her chosen driveway and rang the bell of the small white bungalow.

"Hello there, I'm Sophie Bickerstaff," she said politely, stepping back as an elderly lady appeared from behind the door. She didn't want to appear pushy. "I dropped a leaflet in earlier this week about installing wifi – did you get it?"

"Wifi? Oh yes, I saw that. Not sure what I'd want with wifi thank you." The elderly lady moved to close the door.

"I see you have grandchildren." Alexa gestured to a strategically placed blue toy spade in the edge of the dirt.

"Well, yes, as it happens, I have three. Where on earth did that come from, I thought I'd cleared them all away."

Lonely old folks were so predictable. Always forgetful and always wanting to talk about their grandchildren.

"Looks like they enjoy coming over, do you get to see them much?" Alexa smiled. Eye contact. Very important when building rapport.

"Not as much as I'd like, you know how it is, mum and dad always too busy running around."

"We have the same problem with my mum, she's up in Scotland, but the kids love to Skype her. She wasn't too sure about it at first but now she loves being able to see them more often." Alexa dug into her handbag to retrieve her phone. Building rapport lesson two; establish a common interest. "Here, look," she said smiling. "That's my mum with Ashley on the left and Aileen on the right." She scrolled to some photos of an older woman with two children. Heaven knows who they were, Alexa had found them on the internet earlier but they fitted the bill perfectly.

"They look lovely. What's 'Skype' then?"

"It's like a video phone so you can see your grandchildren whenever you want to. I know my mum really misses seeing our two so I set her up with a nice simple system, like I said she wasn't sure about it at all at first but now she absolutely loves it. In fact she loves it so much that I thought I'd set up a small business to allow folks like yourself to re-connect with their families too. Families are so important, don't you think?" Rapport lesson number three; ask them questions they'll answer yes to.

The elderly lady stood and nodded as she looked at Alexa, standing in the sunshine with her phone full of photos. After a moment she smiled "I'm Joyce," she said. "Why don't you come in and tell me all about it over a cup of tea?" Joyce looked to be in her early 70s with white hair and a light floral dress with a pinny tied around her waist. "You'll have to excuse the mess though; I've been doing some baking for the WI."

"Oh that would be lovely, thank you." Alexa followed her inside. The bungalow was an immaculate indicator of an empty life. The kitchen was dated but pristine and the faint smell of lavender and loneliness seeped from the walls.

"Take a seat." Joyce gestured to a small white Formica table in the corner of the kitchen. A pile of freshly baked shortbread was cooling on the side. "How do you take your tea?"

As Joyce prattled on about her late husband and distant children Alexa smiled and nodded, feeling quietly smug. This was too easy, you just had to know your turf, spend time in the neighbourhood, see who had visitors and who didn't. Those with a steady stream of relatives popping in all the time were crossed off the list immediately; she really didn't need a sickeningly devoted daughter getting in her way. No, she knew what she was looking for; the house where the grandkids came for an hour or so on a Sunday afternoon before the parents dragged them away again to do something more fun. A house that was smart and nicely done up by the owner, ideally a lonely old dear who'd clearly got the money to spend on it. Someone precisely like Joyce.

As Joyce put the tea down on the table she moved a "Sorry we missed you" card from the post office. "I've been meaning to pick that up all week," she said. "But I think it's a new slow cooker my daughter ordered for me off the internet and I'm not sure how I'll get it back here."

"I'll nip down and get it for you after I've had my tea," offered Alexa. "It'll only take me 10 minutes in the car."

This was the time to build trust; the fun stuff came later. She didn't mind running a small errand or two, once she'd earned their trust then she could really get to work.

True to her word Alexa picked up the package.

"Oh, this is perfect." Joyce lifted the slow cooker out of the box. "Look, you've been so kind and this Wifi thing sounds ideal for calling the grandkids so I think I'll give it a go. It's about time I got 'with it'! How long will it take to get set up?"

"No time at all," smiled Alexa. "I have everything you need in the car, all ready to go. Tell you what, I can see how much you miss your grand children so I'll do the whole lot for you for £100 – how does that sound?" Alexa waved her hand to quieten Joyce's protestations. "I get all my kit from a small company owned by a good friend of mine who's trying to set up on their own, not like those massive corporations who don't pay their taxes," she said. "It works out a lot cheaper plus it's helping to support the little guy."

At least part of the story was true, Nick was a good friend and was, technically, a small business, but he didn't pay taxes. In fact he didn't pay for any of the kit he sold either. Alexa just handed over the money, Nick gave her the routers and tablets she needed and no-one asked any questions.

Alexa grinned like a Cheshire cat as she stalked back to her car to collect the equipment. This really was too easy. "Here we go," she said as she piled the bits and pieces onto the kitchen table. "We'll have you chatting to your grandkids before tea time."

Alexa worked fast. She knew exactly what Joyce wanted; she wanted something nice and simple with all of the passwords taken care of. Once she'd set that up she showed her around the tablet and all of the other easy things she could do with it, like setting up online ordering with the supermarket and setting up an Amazon account so she could order presents for the grandkids and watch videos of her favourite old films. All she needed was Joyce's bank account details and she'd be sorted.

"Is it safe giving you all these details?" Joyce asked

"Look, I'm not even writing them down. I'm hard pushed to remember what I had for breakfast this morning never mind memorising this little lot." Alexa joked back. Then she put her serious face on "But never, ever, give any of these details to anyone who asks for them by email." She went on to give Joyce a lecture about online security. She'd even had a leaflet printed, complete with the police logo, warning about the importance of online security. "I'm giving you this just so you have everything you need but don't let it scare you off, just don't give anyone else your login details and you'll be absolutely fine."

An hour or so later and Joyce was good to go. Alexa left her with very easy "how to" guide and a business card with a phone number on it in case she had any questions. And that was it. Simple.

"Thank you for sorting all this out for me, it's been so lovely having someone to chat to." Joyce gave Alexa a little hug on the doorstep. "Come and see me anytime, the kettle is always on."

"No problem at all," smiled Alexa. "Your shortbread was beautiful! Say hi to your grandkids for me when you call them later."

Alexa waved as she drove away. She didn't drive far, just to a small quiet car park hidden away behind the library. Her blonde curls tumbled around her shoulders as she peeled off the tight black wig. She slipped off her jacket and replaced it with a nondescript grey hoody before wriggling out of her tight black skirt and smart shoes and replacing them with jeans and trainers. Twisting the rear view mirror again she wiped every trace of make-up off her face and pulled her hair back into a rough bun. She stuffed her discarded clothes into a bin bag, grabbed a fashionable hold-all off the back seat then quickly wiped the car over to take care of finger prints.

On her way to the station Alexa dropped the bin bag of clothes into a charity shop then stopped at The Commodore Inn. She found a corner table, quickly set up her laptop and plugged her headphones into the phone. As she played back the entire conversation she'd secretly recorded with Joyce she made a note of all of her bank account and log in details. Then she got to work. Predictably the phone rang. It was Joyce.

"I'm sorry to bother you so soon but I've had some sort of email from the bank." She sounded worried. "Someone has tried to access my account from a different AP address or something."

"IP address." Alexa corrected

"Oh yes, that's it – what does it mean?"

"Nothing to worry about, it's just a standard automated email they send when you first set up your account – honestly, it's all fine."

"Well, if you're sure..."

"Absolutely, I promise you it's just another security thing; they're just double checking that it's really you. Just press the "OK" button like I showed you and it will be fine."

Alexa hung up the phone and waited, watching her laptop screen. A moment later the final security block cleared and she was into Joyce's account. "£32,561" she whispered "not bad for a day's work." She quickly transferred the money to her own account using a dummy card reader. She hadn't breezed a first from LSE in Business Finance without knowing how to cover her tracks with a few simple online transactions.

Draining her glass she headed for the station and caught the first train south. Her plan was to lay low in Morecambe for a day or two to see what the pickings there were like. On her way from the station to the hotel she dismantled her "pay as you go" phone dropping the remnants into a number of different bins before depositing the car keys down a nearby drain. One car, hired on fake documents, plus one cheap phone, one business card and a few leaflets all in exchange for enough money to keep her going for a month or two. Bargain.

When she arrived at The Midland Hotel something was clearly in full swing. "Big party?" she asked the receptionist as a group of giggling women weaved past.

“Yeah, one of the local law firms is having a year end party; I’ll put you in a room as far away from them as I can so you won’t be disturbed. How are you paying?”

“Cash”

“In that case we’ll need some identification I’m afraid.”

Alexa reached into her bag and handed over her driving licence.

“Thank you...Sophie,” the receptionist smiled as she read the name on the card. "You’re in room 412, it’s on the 4th floor, sea view, far end of the building.”

Alexa looked around. Drunken office parties meant rich pickings. She had planned an early night but drunken lawyers were good sport. She once cleaned out the head of security for a major European bank who, it turned out, was rather more security conscious when he was dressed than when he was undressed. She raced upstairs, changed into the little black dress she kept in her bag for just such eventualities, pulled a comb through her hair, reapplied her makeup and returned to the bar.

No-one cared what anything cost at these events; it was expense account heaven. She knew the game, no-one was stupid enough to pay to sleep with a prostitute but a professional business woman in distress appealed to their male ego and the rest was child's play.

She looked around; in one corner a gaggle of junior lawyers were telling lewd jokes over a bottle of cheap wine; no point targeting them, juniors never carried enough cash to be interesting.

The office goody two shoes breezed past heading for a sober early night, sensible handbag over her shoulder and a predictably beige M&S jacket in her hand. She shouted goodnight to what looked like three of the senior partners, propping up the bar swapping "I've bagged a bigger client than you" stories. Alexa followed the shouts. Bingo. She had found her prey.

She moved into position at the bar, just a few feet away from them, and ordered a gin and tonic. As she drank it she pulled her phone out of her bag and began a fake conversation with her boyfriend, just loud enough for her targets to hear.

"What do you mean you can't get away? I'm sat here at the bar on my own, looking like a right lemon! I'm all tarted up waiting for you... Well, fine then, it's your loss!"

She finished her "conversation", dropped the phone onto the bar with a clatter, sighed loudly and signalled to the barman. "Another G&T, and this time make it a large one!" This was enough for one of the group to look up, catch her eye and smile. She was in.

"Been stood up?"

"Yeah, not for the first time either. Sorry, I don't want to intrude on your evening, you look like you're having fun and I'm not much company right now."

"Nonsense, can't leave a pretty thing like you at the bar all alone, who knows what might happen. Here, I'll pay for that." Her new friend dug his keys out of his pocket and showed them to the barman. "Put it all onto room 127."

At first they all joined in and made polite conversation, commiserating with her situation and trying out their best chat up lines. Eventually one of them fancied his chances and made a move while the others, exchanging knowing nods and winks of approval, made their excuses and drifted away, eagerly awaiting the lurid details over the breakfast table the next morning.

Joe, her companion for the night, was nice enough. Married to his childhood sweetheart from whom he'd predictably grown apart. Alexa quickly tired of his droning on and excused herself to the ladies where she removed her underwear and inhaled a couple of lines of coke; a nasty habit she'd picked up in London but it made nights like this more bearable.

She returned to the bar stool next to her new best friend, swung it around so she was facing him and parted her legs a few inches. "Come on Joe." She placed her hand on his knee and moved it slowly up his leg. "Why don't we finish this conversation over a nightcap in your room?" Joe's colleagues nudged and cheered as he and Alexa disappeared into the lift together.

As soon as she got him back to his room she wasted no time slipping out of her dress, the no underwear thing really moved things along nice and quickly. That's the bonus with the boring married types, they're very easily impressed. She showed him a few moves he wouldn't forget in a hurry and it wasn't long before he was all done and dusted, fast asleep and snoring fit to wake the dead.

Alexa rifled through his things and emptied his wallet; £350 not bad – the macho lads always took plenty of cash to a night out so they could impress their mates. She left him with his wedding ring for practical rather than sentimental reasons; it looked cheap and she didn't want to risk waking him. His Patek Philippe watch on the nightstand, however, was worth a small fortune despite being engraved on the back with the words "To Joe, love you to the moon and back, Annie".

The words ignited an ember deep in Alexa's heart and for a split second the white hot heat of pain flashed through her body leaving an aching vacuum in its wake. An unruly collection of memories collided in her brain before the icy tomb of self-preservation returned.

"That'll teach you to go sleeping around you bastard," she hissed as she slid the watch into her handbag.

Alexa got dressed swiftly and methodically then slipped silently out of the door and into the deserted corridor. She returned to her room for another drink and a long line of coke to flush away the last of the pain. Another lover. Another time. Another life. She leaned her forehead against the cool glass of the window and gazed out across the Morecambe Bay. The moon hung low in the sky and looked close enough to touch. "Love you to the moon and back," she muttered sarcastically "Well let's see about that." She grabbed a jacket and headed downstairs. As she crossed the lobby the night porter gave her a knowing look but walks of shame were only shameful for those with a conscience.

The cool night air swaddled Alexa as she zipped up her jacket and gazed at the enormous moon now almost touching the sea. On the beach she slipped off her shoes and felt the sand, cool and damp, envelop her toes. Memories of childhood holidays swam around her head. "Just one quick paddle." She swayed a little as the alcohol and drugs jockeyed for position in her brain. "*I'm* just going to the moon and back!" she shouted, flinging her arms wide as she swaggered out across the sands and into the inky black darkness of the bay.

MORECAMBE BAY – IN REAL LIFE

The treacherous sands of Morecambe Bay are legendary and have claimed many lives over the years. Before local roads were built the bay was the main crossing point and there were plenty of local guides (often monks) available to help weary travellers on their way. The main danger comes from the speed with which the tide comes in turning 'easy to paddle' channels into raging torrents in just a few moments. On top of that there's the quicksand and the shifting channels which change with every tide.

Every year thousands of pounds are raised for charity from "Cross Bay Walks" where large groups of people are guided safely across the bay. They are certainly an adventure and, although they are flat walks, the soft sand underfoot means they're also tiring, but the experience of standing in the middle of the bay, a mile or so from 'dry land' is one to remember.

TRUTH BE TOLD...

As the they gathered for their pre-hike briefing Gabby surveyed the collection of boots being sported by the hikers she'd be leading for the day: A pair of ancient leather Brashers with gaiters firmly attached, well looked after but clearly with a lot of miles on the clock, a pair of expensive bright red Salewas that looked fresh out of the box and two pairs of matching Aku boots, one pair pristine and the other still clad in the muddy remnants of a recent walk. As she was about to look up another pair of boots joined them; this time a scuffed cheaper high street brand belonging to a breathless and apologising owner.

"I'm so sorry I'm late."

Gabby looked up and smiled. "Not a problem at all, it's only just gone 10 and I was just about to start the pre hike briefing so you're right on time." She took a deep breath, her first guided walk, but they didn't need to know that. "Thank you for coming." Gripping her walking pole tightly to stop her hands from shaking she continued. "As you know today we'll be walking up to Raven Crag behind us." They all turned to look up at the towering rock face above their heads. "But don't worry, I've done this loads of times before and I promise we're going up the easy way."

A few nervous giggles eased the awkwardness.

"We'll start off walking along the road for a short way, so please keep well in and walk in single file. It's not too far and then we'll be on forest tracks for the rest of the day." She smiled and hoped they couldn't hear her heart thumping. "The view from the top is spectacular and the perfect place for our lunch break, then it's a short but steep descent back to this car park." She smiled again. "Now for the really painful part, as we're such a tiny group how about we all introduce ourselves so we know who we're walking with?"

There was a bit of nervous shuffling as everyone looked at each other with no-one wanting to be the first to speak.

"Well, I'll start," the voice came from Mr Brasher boots. "I'm George, I'm retired and I live in Portinscale near Keswick. "I've walked these fells many times but had a fall earlier this year and stuffed my knee so thought I'd ease myself back in with a group outing."

"How's your knee now?" asked Gabby. "The descent is pretty steep but we have all day so please don't feel rushed; take all the time you need."

"My knee's fine now, thank you."

"Do you have any other medical conditions I need to know about?"

"No," George looked her directly in the eye. "Everything else is fine."

"Oh, well, OK then, but if you think of anything do let me know while we're walking."

"I'll go next," the lady next to him spoke up. "I'm Claire and I love going on adventure holidays." She looked down at her bright red boots as she continued. "I did the three peaks challenge last year and next year I plan to do the Camino de Santiago in Spain."

"Wow," said Gabby. "That's quite a trek, are you doing it alone?"

"No, I plan to go with a group." She looked up and smiled. "I spend the rest of my year behind a desk so like to challenge myself when I'm on holiday."

"Sounds like a great plan. Any injuries or anything I need to know about?"

"Nope, nothing, fit as a fiddle."

"Fantastic!"

"I have a few things you need to be aware of."

Gabby turned to look at the latecomer. "Nothing too serious I hope?"

"No, nothing that should cause any problems today. I did my knee in last year and have problems with my wrists but other than that I'm fine. I'm Eve, by the way." Eve tucked her walking poles under her arm and rolled her sleeve up to show her wrist supports. "See? I'm well prepared and I don't like to make a fuss, but just thought you should know."

"Well you certainly look well prepared," said Gabby, noting Eve's backpack stuffed to the brim with a mug hanging from one side and a hat hanging from the other.

"You can't be too careful," she replied. "I like to have all the bases covered.

Gabby became conscious of the straps of her own backpack digging into her shoulders. The outdoors first aid kit, plus group shelter, bivvie bags, flasks of hot water and extra food 'just in case' all weighed a ton. She grabbed the waist strap and began doing it up as she turned to the last pair. "And you must be Colin and Mark."

"I'm Colin, said the fair haired owner of the clean shiny Akus. "And this is my friend Mark." He gestured to his dark haired companion."

"Nice boots." said Gabby

"Thanks," replied Mark. "We got them earlier this week in Keswick. Colin's managed to keep his nice and clean but I always seem to find the mud."

"You could always try cleaning them," replied Colin with a tight smile.

"I told you, I meant to but I forgot! Really, does it matter? They'll get muddy again today anyway."

"Well, they look lovely," interjected Gabby in an attempt to deflect any tensions. "Right everyone, are we ready? Then let's make a start." The group began adjusting their rucksack and clothing ready for the off. "George, as you know the area would you be happy to be my back marker for now?"

George grunted his approval.

"And remember, keep well in along this first stretch, it's a quiet road but better safe than sorry."

As they set off along the road Gabby looked around; she loved this place hidden deep in the heart of the fells. The first glimmers of spring were emerging all around; daffodils dotted the grass verges and wild garlic was just beginning to line the woodland floor. Their breath hung gently in the air as the sun struggled to reach the valley floor. She used the time to mentally go over everything in her backpack for the hundredth time. What if someone fell over? What if someone got sick? What if someone sued her? She squeezed the top of her walking pole. "Stop it!" she hissed at herself.

"I'm sorry?"

Gabby hadn't realised that Eve was quite so close behind her. "Ignore me, I'm just talking to myself."

"Don't worry, I do that all the time. Walking on tarmac is so dull isn't it? Is it much further?"

"No, just around this bend then we're in the forest for the rest of the day."

"Good. The hard terrain isn't good for my knee."

"I thought you said it wasn't too bad?"

"It isn't. Not really. It just doesn't seem to like road walking."

"Oh, well, look, we're here now." Gabby pointed to a large signpost next to a wooden gate. "OK everyone, we need to cross the road here, it looks clear but please double check. We'll regroup for a moment by the gate."

She watched as everyone looked around then crossed over. They congregated by the gate. "Right, that's the dull bit done, it's all forest track from here in." She pointed through the gate. "It's nice and flat at first then we'll begin to climb gradually though the woods. We'll take it steady but if anyone needs to rest at all please just shout." She looked at George. "Are you still OK at the back? We can swap around with someone else if you want?"

"No, I'm fine thank you."

"Okey dokey, let's crack on!"

They filed through the gate and began making their way along the track. Gabby found the rhythmic sound of boots on gravel familiar and comforting. She smiled as the scent of the forest enveloped them and the outside world disappeared. George was at the back chatting to Claire, Colin and Mark were just ahead of them deep in conversation, and Eve fell into step alongside Gabby, the various items dangling from the outside of her rucksack jangled as she walked.

"You certainly *have* got all the bases covered," observed Gabby. "What exactly do you have in there?"

"Well, there's a whistle, bottle opener, penknife and torch – I keep them on the outside in case of emergencies." Eve twisted to try and point to a cluster of keyrings. "Then I've got a set of spare straps for my knee in the top pocket along with all my painkillers."

"Do you need many?"

"Only when it gets really painful, but I don't like to make a fuss."

"Well, just let me know if you need us to slow down or anything."

Was she overdoing the 'look after yourself' part? Was it too much? Should she back off? Gabby began wondering why she ever thought leading walks would be a good idea in the first place. Colin and Mark caught them up.

"Is the pace OK?" she asked, now worried that she was setting off too quickly.

"Yes, it's perfect," said Colin.

"So, how do you two know each other?" asked Gabby.

"Oh, we work together in IT down near London. We started on the same day six years ago and my desk was right next to Mark's for the first two of those."

"And despite all that, we're still friends," chipped in Mark, putting his hand on Colin's shoulder and giving it a squeeze. Colin brushed his hand away causing Mark to scowl.

Eve and Gabby exchanged glances. "Where are you staying?" asked Gabby.

"Oh, just at a B&B in Keswick," said Mark.

"Separate rooms," added Colin.

"Well, as long as you're being well looked after, that's the main thing." Gabby stopped "Are you three OK to carry on while I just check on George and Claire? There's only one track, just stay on it and stop if you're at all unsure."

"Yes, of course. No problem. We'll just keep plodding on," said Eve opening and closing her hand as she examined it.

"You OK?"

"Yes, just my carpel tunnel playing up. I'll be fine," Eve turned to Mark and Colin. "I would say I'll race you to the top but not sure my knees could cope!"

Gabby watched as they carried on ahead then turned to look at George and Claire puffing up the track. "You alright?"

"Yes, yes," said George, waving his hand dismissively. He was panting quite hard. "I'm just a bit unfit after a couple of months out, that's all." He strode past.

"Everyone's going faster than I expected," breathed Claire. "I'm sure it wasn't this quick on the three peaks."

Gabby walked alongside Claire as George took off up the hill after the others. "We can go at whatever pace suits you." She said. "The others can't get lost and they should wait for us where the track splits at the top." They continued on making small talk as they gradually wound their way up through the woods. Eventually they caught up with the others at a large fork in a clearing. A newly laid path snaked up a freshly cleared area behind them then disappeared into more woodland.

“Right,” announced Gabby. “Not far now, just up and over that final ridge." She pointed along the pristine track. “Once we pop out at the top, brace yourself for the views. It’s also nice and sheltered so we’ll have lunch there too.”

Everyone set off together along the track, chattering more comfortably. George didn’t seem to be saying much. “You OK?” she called over.

“Yes. Fine thanks,” he called back. “You carry on, I’m just pacing myself.”

Gabby continued on, twisting and turning to keep tabs on everyone. Eve appeared to be limping slightly. “Is your knee bothering you Eve?”

“No, I went over on my ankle, but I’m fine. Nearly there now aren’t we?”

“Yes, not far at all.”

“Good, I need a rest!”

As they emerged onto the top of the crag Colin and Mark scampered down the rocks to the viewpoint, dumped their packs and started taking photos; Thirlmere valley stretched out below them and Helvellyn loomed large in the east, tiny pockets of snow still flecking the summit ridge. Eve picked her way down, wincing and muttering in pain as she went, before depositing herself on a flat rock with a big sigh and digging a batch of painkillers out of her backpack. Claire appeared at the top of the ridge looking ashen.

“What’s wrong?” asked Gabby

“I don’t like heights!”

“Don’t like heights?”

“Yes. I didn’t think it would be this high!”

Gabby walked over to her. "Look, why don't you sit here, right at the back, you'll be perfectly safe I promise." She guided Claire to a suitable perch a few meters from the others and well away from the edge.

Claire sat down slowly, back pack still on and walking sticks gripped firmly in hand.

"Shall I help you with your backpack?"

"No. I'm fine. I don't want to move just now."

"How did you cope on the three peaks?"

Claire shifted slightly and looked at her, now slightly dusty, red boots. "I only did half of Ben Nevis then spent the rest of the time on the minibus," she confessed. "I felt like such an idiot. I thought I was over it. Now look at me."

Gabby slipped off her back pack then sat down next to her, putting a friendly arm around her shoulders. "Honestly, don't worry, you'll be fine. I promise. Just sit here and get your breath back and I'll..."

Her sentence was cut short by a shout from George who fell down the last six feet of rocks and landed in an awkward heap in the clearing.

"George. George! Are you OK?" Gabby tried not to sound panicked as she desperately recalled her first aid training. She raced over. "Hello. George. Can you hear me?" Gabby knelt down next to him. "Can you tell me what day it is?"

"Wednesday," wheezed George. He tried reaching to his pocket.

"You need to stay still George, what is it you're trying to reach?"

George groaned. Blood began to pour from a nasty cut on his head and his wrist was bent at an odd angle. Gabby raced back to her rucksack, swiftly opened it and grabbed the first aid kit, yanking it open as she ran back to him. "Mark, Colin – get his backpack off then pop yours down behind him to prop him up. Eve, can we have yours too?" Mark and Colin gently removed George's pack then stacked the others behind him sitting him up. "Claire, we'll need yours too to keep his knees in place. Is that OK?"

Claire nodded and, without saying a word, slipped her pack off and handed it to Colin.

"Put it under his knees to keep them bent," directed Gabby. "Now, George, can you tell me what happened?"

"Medicine...in my pocket...angina..." He reached for his jacket pocket.

"OK George, I'll get it for you. This pocket?"

George nodded as Gabby unzipped his pocket and reached out a small white canister. She took off the lid and handed it to him. "Are you OK to do this yourself or do I need me to do it for you?"

"I can do it..." George took the canister, reached up and sprayed a dose into his mouth then closed his eyes and leaned his head back.

Gabby took a large dressing out of the first aid kit and held it against the cut on his head. "Eve, hold this in place for me while I take a look at his arm. Colin, can you dial 999 and ask for Mountain Rescue?"

George opened his eyes. "No Mountain Rescue! I'll be fine in a few minutes. I just need to rest."

"No George, we have to call them, I can't take that risk."

"I'm fine damn it! Just let me rest!"

"It looks like you've broken your wrist and you've got a nasty cut on your head, we are going to need help to get you back to the car."

The spray was doing its work and George was returning to his senses. "I said no! My legs are fine, I can walk down."

Gabby reached out a triangular bandage but as she opened it the wind caught it, whipping it out of her hands and over the edge of the crag. Claire whimpered a little and shuffled further back on her seat.

"Now what?" asked Mark.

Gabby stood up, "Come with me." She walked over to her rucksack, still behind Claire. Mark followed. "I'm pretending to rummage through here looking for something to tie his arm up with," she whispered, digging around in her pack. "I need you to go and call Mountain Rescue then come back and help us to keep George still until they get here. I can't imagine he's going to make this easy for us."

Mark nodded. "What do I tell them?"

"Tell them we're on the top of Raven Crag with an older gentleman who's had an angina attack. Tell them he's fallen and banged his head but it's under control and that he also appears to have a broken wrist." Gabby pulled a fleece out of her bag. "Then come back as quickly as you can. We'll need some extra layers too to help keep him warm." She pulled out the group shelter. "I can't imagine he'll let us use this, but it's worth a go. We might need your help too Claire." Claire nodded.

Mark wandered up over a nearby rocky outcrop while Gabby returned to George. Eve and Colin were crouched either side of him talking to him gently.

"How are you feeling George? Do you still know what day it is?" asked Gabby.

"Wednesday. For god's sake hurry up, I'm freezing!"

"Do you have any chest pain? It's been 5 minutes so you can take another dose if you need to." Gabby shook out the spare fleece. "I'm going to use this to make a sling so your arm will be more comfortable." She began tying a knot in the fleece to fashion it into a makeshift sling while George took another spray of his angina medicine. "Why didn't you tell me about the angina George?"

"Because it's none of your damned business, that's why!" he snapped.

"OK, let's not worry about that now. Can you lean your head forward for me while I just tie this knot behind your neck?" George leaned forward as Gabby pulled the sling nice and tight. "How's that? Not too tight?"

"It's fine. Now can we go?"

Mark reappeared and gave Gabby a very small nod.

"How's the cut doing?" she asked Eve.

"Not too bad, but I think it's beginning to leak a bit."

Gabby delved back into her first aid kit and produced another dressing, placing it on top of the first. "Keep the pressure on these while I tie them on," she instructed. "George, I'm going to finish bandaging your head, then we need to have something to eat and drink before we can move you. Will that be OK? I have a shelter we can all get into if you're feeling cold."

"No, I'll be fine. Just get a move on!"

Everyone reached their sandwiches and flasks. Gabby stayed close to George and did her best to keep him talking while they ate. She even managed to persuade him to drape a couple of coats around his shoulders and have a few sips of tea. Mark and Colin sat huddled together a short distance away talking quietly and Eve had gone to join Claire to keep her company.

"Oh for god's sake I've had enough of this!" George started moving, trying to stand up.

"You need to stay put until we're all ready to leave!" snapped Gabby.

"Why can't we go now? Why are you all taking your time?"

"We're not taking our time, if we don't eat and drink properly someone else could fall and then where would we be?" Gabby looked him in the eye. "I'm responsible for everyone here and we will wait and go when everyone is ready. Is that clear?"

George glared back. "You've phoned them haven't you?"

"I promise I have not phoned anyone. How could I? I've been with you the entire time!" She looked down and fiddled with the stopper in the top of her flask.

"Tell me about your family." Colin jumped in to rescue the conversation.

"Wife died, kids live miles away. Never see the grandkids. What else do you want to know?"

"How about your hobbies?" tried Mark. "What do you enjoy doing, apart from walking?"

George drew breath as if to answer, then paused. "Nothing really. Walking is all I have." He stared straight ahead. "And now it looks like I can't even do that."

Gabby looked at him, surprised by this new tone to his voice. "What makes you say that?"

"Damned angina. Look at me. I'm nothing but a bloody nuisance."

"You're not a nuisance, but if you'd told me about the angina beforehand then we could have paced ourselves differently, or taken a different route." She offered him another drink of tea. "Why didn't you say something?"

"Because I hate feeling bloody old, that's why." Tears pricked George's eyes. "I used to run up and down all these hills. Done them all. Even did the Bob Graham. Did it in 23 hours 46 minutes. I was bloody fit once you know."

"But you can't help getting old, or sick. We are what we are," said Colin

"Yes, we are, aren't we?" added Mark, acidicly, staring at Colin.

"And what the hell is going on with you two?" barked George, returning to form. "You've been bickering like old women all day."

"We've been dating for three years, but Colin still won't tell his parents. They think he's shacked up with some tart called Mandy."

"For god's sake we've been over this!" spat Colin. "They're old, they're Catholic, they won't understand!"

"You just don't care enough about me, that's the problem. You're ashamed to be gay."

"This is neither the time nor the place for this conversation. Our focus right now should be on keeping George comfortable until Mountain Rescue gets here." As soon as he said it Colin's hand flew to his mouth. "Oh I am SO sorry," he muttered.

George groaned and leaned his head back. "It's OK. I guessed you'd called them. I worked with the team for 20 years, that's why I didn't want you calling them, it's too embarrassing."

"Sorry," said Gabby. "Truth be told, it's my first ever guided walk and I just needed to do what was best. I can't lose someone on my first ever walk now, can I?"

"But you said you'd done this loads!" Eve looked annoyed.

"I've been up Raven Crag loads of times, I just haven't led a group up here before. To be honest, I'm not sure I will again, it's been more of an adventure than I imagined."

George laughed. "I've not really helped have I? But don't be put off you did great. If you don't believe me just ask this lot."

As he finished speaking a team of four brightly clad Mountain Rescue volunteers emerged from the woods. The leader strode over to the group huddled on the ground. "What have you been up to George? Not causing trouble I hope?"

"I'm fine, thanks to this young lady." He smiled at Gabby.

"I am *so* glad to see you" she said. "I've done my best to patch him up and keep him comfortable."

"It looks like you did a great job, love the improvised sling, very clever."

"Excuse me." Eve interrupted from her perch. "I don't mean to but in, but my knee has been playing up again. Are you able to take a look at it? I mean, I don't want to make a fuss or anything..."

RAVEN CRAG – IN REAL LIFE

Raven Crag is offers one of the best viewpoints in the Lake District. Thirlmere Reservoir was built in the late 19th century after a protracted battle. There had originally been two smaller lakes in the valley with a very pretty crossing point known as the 'Celtic Bridges' at the pinch point between the two. Water runs from the reservoir along the Thirlmere Aqueduct all the way down to Manchester, over 100 miles away. It flows entirely by gravity with no pumping stations along the route. An ornate fountain marks the ceremonial end of the pipeline in Albert Square, central Manchester.

The 'Bob Graham' is a popular ultra long distance run which involves running 66 miles over 42 fells in under 24 hours. The route taken by the walkers in the story is a lovely hike with a long, gradual, ascent. You can either return the same way or take the shorter, much steeper, descent through the woods in front of the crag. And if you go on a guided walk, do please tell the walk leader of any pre-existing medical conditions.

THE GREAT ESCAPE

Sketching the managing partner with devil's horns and carrying a trident was therapeutic. As the meeting progressed the drawing became more elaborate until by 'any other business' it had evolved into a fire breathing devil surrounded by a dozen or so minions, all of whom bore a striking resemblance to the equity partners. The autumn sunshine streamed in through the dust coated windows and from where he was sitting Nigel could see the beautiful domed roof of Manchester Central Library. A few people were sitting on the benches around the outside enjoying a coffee and a pastry in the autumnal sunshine and Nigel looked at them enviously.

Tall, with short cropped dark hair (slightly greying and slightly thinning if he was honest) and still just about on the slim side of middle age, Nigel brushed a few stray biscuit crumbs from his expensive dark blue suit and shifted his gaze to his ludicrously expensive Italian leather shoes. His mother has always said *"in this life you need good shoes and a good bed because if you're not in one, you're in the other."* For what this pair cost they should last him right through this life and well into the next. The only concession to his more artistic persona was his collection of ties, many of which had caught the attention of Eric, the managing partner, a man whose lack of imagination was perfectly complemented by his humourless demeanour.

"Is there a carnival in town?" he'd ask dryly, whenever Nigel wore one of his brighter creations

Nigel clenched his teeth at the thought. He imagined Eric's home decorated in a palate of greys and browns and envisioned him admonishing his wife for their grass being ever so slightly too green.

Returning to his desk after the meeting Nigel slumped into his chair with a sigh.

"Fun was it?" Jean, his secretary, wandered in with a pile of papers for him to sign.

"Another two hours of my life I'll never get back," he replied, reaching for his pen. "What are this lot?"

"Top one is the Perkins file, he's been chasing for an update." She handed him the document. "The challenges of being a big city lawyer eh? How are Abbie and the kids? Back from the US yet?"

"Yes, came back yesterday." Nigel flicked through the long letter giving it a cursory glance before signing it, Jean had been his secretary for over 20 years and he trusted her implicitly. "Another family holiday I missed and another batch of photos I won't be in. Is this Mrs Heaton's file? Have the hospital finally sent their report through?" He reached for a large manila envelope.

"Yes, at long last. Is James more settled now?" She handed over the hospital report then neatly folded the first letter and slotted it into an envelope.

Nigel sighed. "Not great to be honest; still acting up at school. Most of it lands on Abbie's shoulders but I should be around more to help." He paused for a moment, pen in mid air.

"Don't beat yourself up; you've had enough on your plate lately with everything going on here, plus all the running around looking after John." Jean sat down and looked at Nigel. "What time's the funeral?"

"2pm. My kid brother and still Eric insisted I come in for the partner's breakfast meeting and not take the whole day. I know his retirement and the merger are a big deal but one day is all I wanted."

"I know. Look, I've cleared your diary, just sign these and you're done."

"He had the right idea though."

"Who did?"

"John."

"How so?"

"He ducked out of the rat race. He got his first from Oxford like me and Keith but then instead of going into corporate servitude he took off travelling." Nigel picked up a photo on his desk and handed it to Jean, his thumb left a print on the smart chrome frame. "That's him in Nepal. We always teased him about it and mum and dad never really understood it, but I've always been rather jealous of him."

"How's his wife taking it?"

"Ellen? She's a tough old cookie but it's been a gruelling few months for her. Cancer treatments aren't pretty."

Jean picked up another document and passed it over the desk. "This is just a requisition for a new laptop for Derek, he dropped his last one and smashed the screen. It's the last one to sign I promise."

"John would have been able to fix that." Nigel studied the document before signing it. "He ran his own IT company in Barrow. He loved it. He looked after lots of small businesses and everybody knew him."

"Right, that's all the paperwork done." Jean swept all the documents up into a neat pile. "You need to take off now to collect Abbie before the funeral. I'm sure we can manage without you for a few hours."

"Do you know what one of the most depressing things to buy is?" He asked, leaning on his desk and looking across at Jean. "An annual season ticket. Knowing that you're just going to be going to and from the same place every single day for an entire year. That's not a job, it's a prison sentence."

"Why don't you take some time off?" Jean smiled and put her hand on his arm. "Ignore Eric, you need to look after yourself."

"Yes, I know. I'm supposed to be his favourite so I may as well cash in on that. Could be career suicide even so. Thanks for all your help – don't know what I'd do without you." He smiled as he stood up and slipped on his coat. "Can you sort my desk out for me?"

"Of course. Give my love to Abbie," replied Jean as he headed out of the door.

Nigel stared blankly out of the window as the train made its way up to Lancaster, the landscape slipped past with monotonous familiarity. He picked his car up from the station then collected Abbie, an investment manager for an international bank, from her smart city centre office.

"Will Keith and Diane be there?" asked Abbie, as they navigated the one way system.

"Keith's flying up but Diane said she couldn't get time off." Nigel glanced across at her. "Be nice to him. I know you don't like him, but John was his kid brother too."

"It's not that I don't like him, it's just that I never know what to say to him." She pulled the visor down and checked her lipstick in the mirror. "He only ever talks about work and has zero sense of humour."

"It's how we were brought up. He's a lot like dad. He's still my big brother though." The lights changed as Nigel put the car into gear and pulled away. "My only brother now."

"I know. Sorry." Abbie put the visor back up and placed her hand gently on Nigel's leg. They continued the drive north in comfortable silence.

The service was at Holy Trinity church in Bardsea, an imposing building with breathtaking views across Morecambe Bay; there was a chill in the autumn air but the sky was blue and the weak rays of sun brought a welcome edge of warmth to the day. The place was packed; John was clearly well known and liked in the community and Ellen was surrounded with people offering their condolences. "They keep telling me 'it's what he would have wanted'," she said, when she had a moment alone with Nigel. "But he didn't want to be dead. He loved days like this."

Nigel gave her a big hug. "I know. They just don't know what else to say."

Keith arrived and came over to join them. "How are you doing?" He looked at Ellen.

"Hanging in there and wishing this had never happened." Tears ran down her face.

Keith shifted uncomfortably while Nigel fished around for a hanky, one arm still around her shoulders. "Here you go, I think we need to go in and take our seats."

Ellen nodded and they filed inside to the front pew. The sun poured through the stained glass windows in the apse flooding the church with multicoloured light. Ellen's eyes were fixed on the coffin throughout and her lips barely moved during the hymns.

Nigel tried to avoid looking at the casket, topped with one simple wreath from Ellen; if he didn't look at it then maybe John wasn't dead. He shouldn't be alone up there all alone, John hated being on his own in front of a crowd. Nigel forced himself to look. Flecks of dust hung in the air, slow dancing in the narrow shafts of sunlight.

Following the funeral everyone was invited to The Stan Laurel Inn in Ulverston for the wake; it was one of John's favourite places. There was a large table of food at one end and small circular tables covered in crisp white cloths arranged around the room. Most people were standing and chatting and the air was filled with the low hum of sombre words. Nigel and Abbie sat alone at one of the tables. At odds with the solemn mood a film photo of Laurel & Hardy hung on the wall above their heads. As they talked Nigel studied her face; there were a few traces of grey in her auburn hair but she was still as beautiful as when they first met at university and bonded over a shared love of The Damned.

Nigel took a deep breath. "I think it's time I did something different."

"Different how?" Abbie put her fork down and looked at him.

"I want to paint, I want to create, I'm done with aeroplanes and hotel rooms – I want to do something that means something to other people not bores the pants off them." He paused to take a sip of his tea. "I want to see my kids more, I want to be at home, I want to help them find their own passion, not feel pushed into the corporate machine like I did – I want to tell people what I do without them dozing off half way through the conversation."

"You've said all of this before, so what do you want to do about it this time?"

"Honestly? I want to sell the house, maybe head back to near your parents place in Ayr and open an art gallery."

"What sort of gallery?"

"Paintings, ceramics, that kind of thing; local artists mainly and maybe even a few of my own pieces. I always wanted to study art but dad wouldn't let me." He put his cup down. "We could keep a broader appeal by stocking cards, gifts and artistic materials to entice more people in and set up a website so we're not reliant on people visiting the gallery."

"You sound like you've given this a lot of thought." She paused and looked at him. "I'm not sure Ayr is the right place for something like that, how about Glasgow – it's only 40 minute drive from Ayr and there are some lovely areas around the edge of the city which could work perfectly?"

Nigel looked at her for a moment. "You mean you'd actually consider it?"

"Well, you've not been happy for a while now have you? And when was the last time we had a proper family holiday without one or other of us spending at least a day of it fielding calls from the office or catching up on our emails around the pool?"

"What do you know about running an art gallery?"

"Not a lot, but if I can navigate the bank through the crisis of the past five years I'm sure I can pick it up. How do you plan to finance it?"

"We should do alright from selling the house. I know we won't get as much for it as we would have five years back, but we should still make a decent profit." He pushed a few crumbs around the table with his fingers as he spoke. "Plus if we change the kids to day pupils, rather than boarders, that would save us a fair bit too. I never thought you'd be up for something like this." He smiled at her.

"Well, your parents are gone, mine are desperate to see more of us and the kids and with Jimi still playing up we really do need to spend more time with them." She leaned back in her seat and looked across the room to where her bereaved sister-in-law was sitting. "And after what's happened to John and Ellen, this seems the perfect time to do something new."

Keith came over and sat down placing a plate of sandwiches on the small table in front of them. "I never know what I'm supposed to do at these things," he said as he lifted a sandwich and took a bite.

"I was just saying to Abbie that I think it's time I packed in the whole lawyering thing and headed north so we can spend more time with the kids."

"You can't be serious," spluttered Keith, mouth still half full of food.

"I'm deadly serious. You know I always wanted to study art at uni but dad wouldn't let me. Said he'd refuse to pay my tuition fees if I didn't study law."

Keith swallowed his mouthful. "And he was right. A law degree is a lot more use than an art degree. You were the youngest partner in your firm's history. You couldn't have done all that with a pot of paints."

"I know, but I never took to corporate life like you did. I kept my end of the bargain and I've served my time, now I want to do something I love for a change."

"I think I'll leave you two to this," said Abbie, excusing herself. "I'm going to see how Ellen's doing."

"You might 'hate lawyering'," retorted Keith "But you don't hate the pay packet – I saw your flashy Merc out there. Remember what dad used to say?"

"'Artists can only afford to eat after they're dead' – yes, I remember, but things are different now."

"Are you sure this isn't just another one of your flights of fancy? It would mean the end of all the nice designer clothes and posh meals out. And no more foreign holidays either." Keith was warming to his theme.

"I hardly see the kids these days and Jimi has been acting up at school so we need to do something. You don't have kids; you don't know what it's like trying to juggle it all." Nigel spat out the last part and instantly regretted it.

Keith glared at him. "That wasn't our choice, but thank you for reminding me, infertility so easily slips the mind," he added sarcastically.

"Look, I'm sorry." Nigel's voice softened. "I just think it's time I did something different."

"This is just one of those grief things. We'll both miss John but that doesn't mean we should turn our lives upside down."

Nigel's phone buzzed in his pocket. He took it out and looked at the flashing screen.

"Who is it?" asked Keith

"Work. Eric." sighed Nigel. "They can't leave me in peace for one afternoon!"

"It must be important then mustn't it? Are you going to take it?" They looked at each other. "Are you going to tell him you're off to follow your heart? Or are you going to do the right thing and keep your head down. You know you'll be the one to step into Eric's shoes when he retires and then you'll be head of your own firm."

Nigel stared down at his phone, his thumb poised over the flashing green icon.

"Well?"

BARDSEA – IN REAL LIFE

Holy Trinity Church in Bardsea is in a prominent location with spectacular views out across Morecambe Bay. It was built in 1843 and is noted for its magnificent stained glass windows. Immediately behind the church is Birkrigg Common with a rare double stone circle and more gorgeous views.

The Stan Laurel Inn in Ulverston is named in honour of Stan Laurel who was born in the town on 16th June 1890. He only lived there for a few years but came back to visit regularly throughout his childhood and often spoke of his fond memories of the town. There are many other tributes to the town's favourite son including the excellent Laurel and Hardy museum and the florist in the market square named "Floral and Hardy".

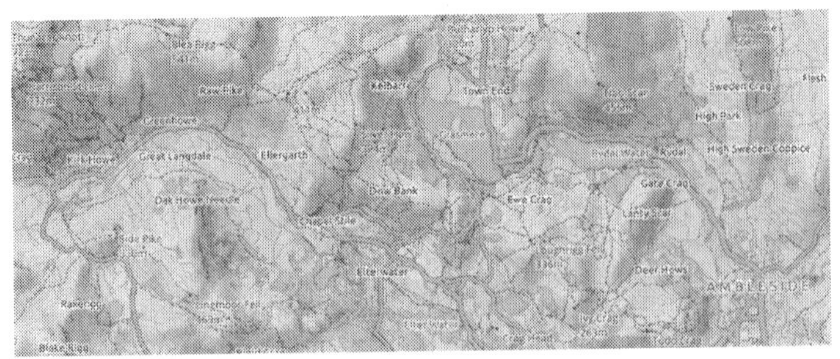

BIRDS OF A FEATHER

"Morning! Two returns to Dungeon Ghyll please," beamed the passenger. Tourist. Gavin hated tourists. Seeing happy relaxed people day after day while he was hard at work really ground him down. At least when he'd driven busses around Manchester the passengers had had the decency to look as miserable as he was.

"£12.50" grunted Gavin.

"Lovely day for it!"

"Hmmm."

"I'll bet this is the prettiest bus route in the country, you're so lucky getting to see this all year round."

"Hmmm." Gavin's perky new friend was showing no signs of taking their tickets so Gavin handed them to him and fixed his eyes on the road ahead. The next passenger boarded.

"Two returns to Dungeon Ghyll please – gorgeous day isn't it?"

Gavin tried to force a smile. He'd been on an "Excellent Customer Care" course where they told him that they were not passengers they were customers and he had to be nice to them, but he didn't see why. There were no other buses along this route, if someone wanted to get from Ambleside to Dungeon Ghyll on the bus they had to take his bus, so they should just be grateful it was running at all. He was a bus driver, paid to drive a bus and that is exactly what he was doing. Anything else wasn't in his job description.

A group of elderly locals tried boarding with their passes. "Not valid 'til 9:30." Gavin stared at them, daring them to quibble.

"But it's 9:24 – can't you make an exception?"

"No. The system won't let me."

"But we want to get an early start on our group ramble."

"Well you can get on the bus but you'll have to pay full fare like everyone else, or wait for the 10:24."

They all stared at each other for a moment before Gavin again returned to looking at the road ahead. He liked staring at the tarmac, it never answered back.

"It's no good," said the group leader loudly addressing his group as he left the bus. "This miserable sod won't let us on so we'll go and have a nice cup coffee and a cake and get the next one."

"How much is a return to Dungeon Ghyll please?" The very polite request came from a young woman, maybe mid to late 20s. She was clad head to toe in outdoor gear which had seen better days, with a scarf haphazardly poking out of the top of her jacket and strands of straight dark hair escaping from her woolly hat. She pushed her glasses back up her nose. "How much is a return to Dungeon Ghyll please?" she repeated.

She was an attractive woman but Gavin's attention was focused on the very expensive pair of lightweight Canon binoculars hanging around her neck, completely at odds with the rest of her appearance.

"Sorry, £6.25." He watched as she fiddled in her tiny zip up purse for the right change. "You a bird watcher?"

She flushed slightly, not looking at him as she answered. "Yes, I love birds and I heard there were some interesting ones along the valley." There was a small label with the words "Chloe's Bins" stuck to the binoculars.

Chloe. That was his daughter's name. She still lived in Salford with his ex-wife. Well, technically she was away studying Geology at Southampton University, but it was his ex-wife she went home to, not Gavin. "I've seen a few buzzards along there this week and last weekend spotted a couple of Wheatears up on the track from Stickle Tarn to Dungeon Ghyll," he said, glad at last to meet a kindred spirit.

"I'm hoping to see a Ring Ouzel." She smiled as she handed over the money, still not quite meeting his eyes. "I want to get off at Stickle Barn, if I sit near the front can you shout and tell me when that is please?"

"Of course, there's a big car park there so you can't miss it, but I promise I'll give you a shout."

Chloe took her ticket and quickly found a seat. Gavin watched her in his mirror as she fiddled with the small backpack on her lap then settled to look out of the window. He was very proud of his bus with its smart blue and white livery and, at this time in the morning, the clean fresh smell of detergent wafting up from the recently mopped floor.

He closed the doors and pulled away, his mind now back on the road. As usual the Rothay Bridge over to Clappersgate was a nightmare; only just wide enough for the bus and yet cars coming the other way still insisted on trying to squeeze past. "For god's sake, can't they just wait for one minute!" He hissed quietly to himself. He jabbed the breaks as a white Audi made an ill advised attempt to share the bridge with him.

"Ow!"

Gavin looked in his passenger mirror and saw Chloe rubbing her head. "Sorry!" he shouted down the bus. He glared at the Audi driver then gently swung the bus around the bend and off along the road. He checked his mirror again; she was sitting quite still, hand on the back of the seat in front to steady herself and eyes fixed on scenery slipping past outside the window.

The road was narrow and winding and not helped by the occasional hiker walking along the verge. "Thousands of miles of footpaths in the bloody hills and still they clutter up my road." He kept up his ill tempered commentary as he navigated the twist and turns along the route.

At Skelwith Bridge two of the perky hikers got off and a small family with three border terriers clambered on. A harassed mum shepherded two young children down to the back of the bus while dad, with a baby in a carry sack on his back, tried to pay the bus fares with the three dogs straining at the lead. “Beautiful day for it!” He said, as he handed over the money.

“Hmmm.” Gavin closed the door and pulled away before dad had a chance to get to his seat causing him to stagger along the bus.

One of the dogs darted right and jumped on the seat next to Chloe; she smiled and put out her hand to stroke it. “Hello sweetie,” she cooed.

“Sorry.” said dad, still juggling his wallet and tickets.

“Oi! No dogs on the seats!” shouted Gavin.

“Sorry!” said dad again, this time yanking the lead and lurching into a seat next to the rest of his family.

As the road passed along the side of the River Brathay and the valley opened up around them even Gavin relaxed and smiled a little; it was a lovely day and the fells were looking particularly fine. He spotted a couple of his favourite bird watching haunts and then, as they rumbled over the cattlegrid into Elterwater village, the view along the valley to the Langdale Pikes opened up. The one spot on the entire route that made this job worthwhile;

whatever the time of year the pikes never let him down. Deep lush green in the summer, every shade of gold and bronze in the autumn, dusted with snow through the winter or now, with the late spring sunshine catching the summits, golden and inviting with just a hint of green as the bracken returned for the season.

More people clambered on and off at Chapel Stile; the early buses where the place for clean fresh hikers with backpacks full of food and heads full of excited plans. In the evening he'd be picking them up again, dusty and dirty from their day of adventure and eager to get back into town for beer and food. He checked his mirror. Chloe was still there, sitting in exactly the same position with her eyes glued to the window, but now the fingers on her right hand were tapping and fidgeting as she held the seat in front and a small smile was spreading across her face.

As they passed the Stickle Barn car park, Chloe looked up. "Not yet" shouted Gavin, "It's better if I drop you off in a couple of minutes on my way back through." She smiled and nodded and her eyes returned to the window. At the head of the valley Gavin expertly turned the bus around in the entrance to The Old Dungeon Ghyll and paused to deposit a gaggle of hikers and the family with the dogs.

"Thank you so much, have a lovely day!" They all chattered and laughed as they clustered along the road sorting out backpacks and detangling leads from legs. Gavin ignored them, closed the door and drove off.

He returned along the lane to the Stickle Barn where he pulled the bus into the car park and stopped the engine.

Chloe got up to get off. "Thank you." she smiled.

"Do you know where you're heading?" asked Gavin

"Erm...no...not really. I thought I might walk out along the valley floor and loop back around."

"Well, if you're after the Ring Ouzel you'll need to head up higher

– there's a good path from the back of the carpark." He pointed towards a row of parked cars "There's a gate just behind those cars and it'll lead you up to Stickle Tarn, from there bear left and look for the path across to Dungeon Ghyll, there are some great views from a spot called Pike Howe."

Chloe smiled again. "Thank you, I might just give that a go."

"Either way there are some useful maps and information on that board up by the barn."

"That's good to know. I'll go and have a look." she answered politely then got off the bus and walked up the car park to the information boards.

After a short rest Gavin sighed and swung his bus back out onto the road. "What fresh hell awaits me now?" he muttered as he pulled away, swearing loudly at a Toyota Prius trying to navigate into a layby.

The day passed without further incident, apart from a group of 3 lycra clad cyclists who all wanted to bring their bikes on board, a small child vomiting on one of the seats and an American couple trying to pay their fare with a fifty pound note.

Just after lunch Gavin was approaching Chapel Stile on his way back to Ambleside with an empty bus when he saw Chloe standing in the middle of the road, one arm waving furiously to flag him down and the other wrapped around a large bundle of some sort. He pulled up sharply next to her and she jumped on chattering so quickly he struggled to make sense of it all.

"You have to help, I found this poor thing in a field over there, I know you said to go up to the tarn but I don't like heights, so I walked along the valley floor and then I found him in a field, well it looks like he flew into a fence, or got clipped by a car or something, either way he can't fly and we have to help him." Her words tumbled out in a breathless rush.

"What? Who? Where?" Gavin looked confused.

Chloe moved the top of the bundle under her arm to reveal the smooth speckled head of a buzzard. He was wrapped in her down jacket and, despite being injured, was clearly not happy at being restrained. His dark inquisitive eyes darted around and his powerful beak tried to peck at Chloe's arms.

Oh my goodness, he's stunning!" exclaimed Gavin "I've never seen one so close up before – just look at his feathers!"

"Never mind his feathers, we need to get him to a vet, do you know where we might find one?"

"There's one in Ambleside. How on earth did you catch him?"

"I think he's broken his wing. He can't fly so I threw my jacket over him. He keeps clawing at it and trying to peck me. How quickly can we get there?"

"Go and sit down, hold on tight and make sure you keep him safe."

Gavin closed the doors, waited for Chloe to take her seat then he put his foot down. The engine revved, startling three Herdwick ewes chewing the grass along the verge and causing them to scatter up onto the nearby hillside. The bus lurched along the lane and Chloe braced herself as they swung around a sharp left hand bend and down in Chapel Stile. Gavin checked his mirror again and watched as she soothed the bird. "Shhh, shhh, it's OK, we're trying to help." She stroked the top of the buzzard's head with her finger as she tried to keep him calm.

"Bugger!"

"What?"

"Passengers!"

"Can they wait?"

"They'll have to!" Gavin tried gesticulating to the bird and Chloe in the bus as he raced past the stop, recognising the group of elderly hikers he'd refused to let on earlier. "Really not your day is it?" he muttered as he sailed past, watching them shouting and waving in his rear view mirror.

Roaring through Elterwater the bus screeched to a halt, launching Chloe from her seat, her arms remaining tight around the precious bundle. "Oowwwww!"

"You OK?"

"Yeah, just banged my head. What's the problem?" She shuffled back up onto her seat.

"Some idiot in a 4 wheel drive scared to take the damned thing off the road." replied Gavin. He leaned out of the window. "Oi, mate, they've taken those things up Everest, I think it can cope with a muddy field, now get off the sodding road!" He hooted his horn angrily then moved the bus out and around the car before putting his foot down and pulling up the hill out of the village as quickly as he could. "How's he doing?"

"Fine I think. Still trying to peck me so I think that's a good sign!"

The bus tilted and swayed as Gavin pushed it along the narrow lanes. This time he was ignoring the views and all his attention was on the road ahead. They began to drop down towards Skelwith Bridge. "No, no, no, no no!"

"What now?"

"Tractor. Please go to Coniston, please go to Coniston, please go to Coniston."

"What?"

"I'm hoping he turns right to Coniston at the big junction ahead, if not, we'll never get past him. Go on, go on, go on...YES!"

The tractor ahead turned right towards Coniston and Gavin hurled the bus out in front of a motorhome. "Don't want to get stuck behind one of those idiots either!"

Chloe looked up to see the motorhome driver and her passenger shouting and waving angrily at the bus as Gavin turned it along the main road.

"You'd never guess this is an old Roman Road" Gavin shouted "I thought they were all supposed to be bloody straight!" The bus screeched around two more bends startling a group of hikers who quickly scrambled over a nearby wall to safety. A lorry appeared around the bend ahead, flashing his lights at Gavin to slow down. Gavin was having none of it and threw the bus into the small, 'only marginally larger than a bus'-sized gap. CRUNCH! "Bugger."

"You OK?"

"Yes, but the wing mirror's gone. Not too much further now though!" He put his foot down and tree branches scraped and squealed along the side of the bus as he forced it through the remainder of the gap and on towards the town. "Don't even think about it!" he shouted out the window at a BMW trying to squeeze past him on Rothay Bridge. "Nearly there now. Damn it! Are you any good at running?" The bus ground to a halt next to the park.

"Sorry?"

"The traffic ahead is solid, someone's blocking the road, our best bet is for you to run up to the vets." Chloe gathered up her bundle and joined Gavin at the front of the bus. He pointed in front "That road dead ahead is Church Street and the vets is up there, about halfway along on the left hand side, opposite the art gallery. You go on and I'll get to you as quickly as I can."

Chloe nodded and jumped off the bus. Gavin watched as she half jogged along the pavement, talking to the buzzard in her arms the whole way. Several people stopped to turn and see what she was carrying but she kept on going. He watched as she disappeared into the vets.

Gavin continued cursing and muttering as the traffic inched forwards. Eventually he got past the badly parked white van, turned right and lurched to a halt at the bus stop. He changed the sign on the front of the bus to read "Out of Service". "Sorry folks," he said to the group of passengers readying themselves to board. "Family emergency."

He jumped down to the pavement, raced across the carpark, along the side street and into the vets. Chloe was sitting in the waiting room alone.

"Where's the bird? Is he OK?"

"He's going to be fine." A male voice came from behind Gavin. He swung around to see a smiling tunic-clad vet. Chloe jumped to her feet. "We've made him as comfortable as we can but we'll need to operate to fix that wing."

"What then?" asked Chloe.

"Well, then we'll send him to a local bird sanctuary to recover, but thanks to your swift actions he should be right as rain again in a few months."

Chloe and Gavin smiled and Gavin put his arm around Chloe's shoulders giving her a hug. "Well done," he whispered. "How does it feel to be a life saver?"

Chloe grinned. "I couldn't have done it without you."

They both thanked the vet and wandered outside back towards the bus stop. Gavin looked at Chloe and noticed a sore looking bump on her forehead "I am really sorry about your head. Are you OK? Do we need to find you a doctor?"

Chloe put her hand up and ran her fingers gently over the lump. "No, I'm fine; it'll be gone in a day or so. It really wasn't your fault."

"Well, if you're sure..." Gavin's mobile rang. He fished it out of his pocket. "Bugger!"

"What's wrong?"

"It's my boss. I might have some explaining to do." They stood next to each other in the car park looking at the scratched and battered remains of Gavin's bus.

"Is he a bird lover?"

"I think I'm about to find out."

LANGDALE VALLEY – IN REAL LIFE

The Langdale Valley is a very popular spot and the starting point for dozens of interesting walks. The National Trust Car Park at Stickle Barn is large and free if you're an NT member or the area is well served with a local bus from Ambleside (and most of the drivers are a lot friendlier than Gavin!).

Whatever your level of expertise there will be something to suit you in the valley from a nice flat family stroll along the valley floor to a full on climbing expedition up the surrounding crags. The most popular route is up to Stickle Tarn and there are steady stream of people along here all year around. For something a little different you could try taking a walk up The Band where there's a great bench to sit and enjoy the views along the valley.

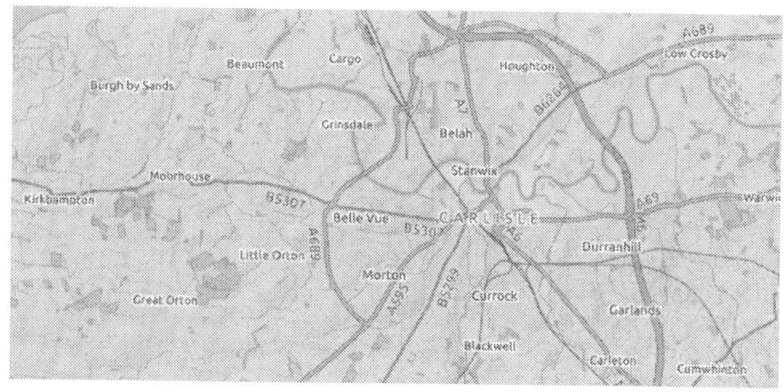

US VERSUS THE WORLD

"Tomatoes, I can't even get proper tomatoes." Claudio muttered to himself as he peered down at the contents of his shopping trolley. Six perfect red spheres all neatly displayed in their taut cellophane wrapper stared back. He longed for big, juicy, misshapen tomatoes like his Uncle Mauritzio used to grow. Granted they may not have looks so pretty but they dripped with flavour and the juices swam around the plate after a meal just waiting to be mopped up with a big chunk of fresh baked ciabatta. His phone buzzed . A text from Manuela.

"See if you can get any aubergines while you're in there – and don't forget the baby wipes. xxx"

Claudio sighed and slid the phone back into his pocket without replying.

He had been spoiled with food as a child, and wine. Growing up on a vineyard in the heart of the Chianti wine region meant he'd been drinking wine from a very young age. He could tell the good from the bad and knew when he was about to get ripped off. He didn't look much like a wine connoisseur; average height and build with hair which was a bit on the long side. Since the baby had come along he was working all the hours god sent and hadn't had time to get it cut. Jeans and a grubby t-shirt replaced the latest fashions he used to sport.

As he surveyed the wine aisle he paused to inspect several bottles of Chianti – he knew the owners of the vineyards and used to play hide and seek in their fields when he was a child. He smiled as happy memories seeped from the bottles and into his mind. Long summer evenings chasing around the vines; evenings were the perfect time for burning off excess energy after the stifling heat of the day. Claudio could still picture the faces of all of his childhood friends and smell the hot earthy dryness of the soil; he smiled as he remembered the clip round the ears from his mama for the dusty red stains etched deep into his knees and clothes.

"Which one should we get?" A couple next to him were staring in bewilderment at the hundreds of wines in front of them.

"No idea, how about this?" The man reached out, picked up a bottle of Gallo wine and began studying the label.

"Don't get that one!" Claudio couldn't help himself. He hated Gallo wines.

The couple looked at him in surprise. "Whyever not?"

"Well, for a start it's mass produced and lacks any character but also the owners of the Gallo company sued the Consorzio of Chianti Classico to stop them using the words 'Gallo Nero'." The couple looked somewhat surprised but were far too polite to interrupt. Claudio took the bottle from them, turning it around to show the label on the back as he continued his tirade. "Our symbol has always been a black rooster, 'gallo nero' in Italian, but they sued us and said it was their name and now we can't use it on our bottles. How could a group of poor famers fight those American bullies?" He replaced the offending bottle, reached down and picked up a bottle labelled 'Farmers Wine' from the bottom shelf. "Here," he said, handing it to them. "I used to play on this vineyard as a child; the wine is cheap but better than anything else on the shelves."

"Thank you." They looked a little unsure as they took the bottle from the ranting Italian but Claudio wandered off before they had chance to ask any questions.

At the checkout his cheeks reddened as he handed over a couple of special offer coupons clipped from the local paper and he tried not to catch the eye of the cashier as he counted out the exact money. The shopping weighed heavy as he trudged to the bus stop. The bus was late, already crammed with standing room only. It was full of people heading home from the office, most of them lost in their phones or occasionally gazing out of the window. Claudio still had a long late shift ahead of him and would be lucky to get home before 1am. He sighed leaning his head against the pole he was hanging on to. It was hot, it was stuffy and he was fed up. Each time the bus stopped the people getting on and off knocked against him forcing him to corral the bags with his feet to stop them toppling over.

"Why do you never answer my texts? Did you get the baby wipes?" Manuela pounced on him as he walked through the door.

"Of course, yes!" he replied tersely. "Give me chance to unpack the bags before you start on me."

Manuela came fussing over rifling through the bags and putting things away into the tiny cupboards of their studio flat. There was very little room to fit anything in the cupboards; in fact there was very little room to fit the three of them within the cramped four walls. It was all they could afford and it was grim. After bumping into each other several times Claudio gave up and slumped down on the sofa bed; he wanted to help but sometimes he felt like a visitor in his own home. Manuela deftly slotted things away, straining to reach the higher shelves but never once asking for help. The kitchen, if you could call it that, was her domain.

Tucked away in the basement of an old Victorian house in an unfashionable corner of Carlisle they lived in one room with a bay window below street level and a tiny bathroom. The place was immaculate but the walls were a faded shade of off white and there was a patch of damp around the bottom of the window that the landlord assured them had been dealt with. Claudio wasn't convinced; he was worried that it would affect the baby. As people passed by on the pavement above they sometimes glanced down and occasionally tossed their litter into the laughingly labelled "courtyard" outside.

Their few mismatched hand-me-down possessions were neatly arranged on a tired looking carpet worn thin with their tracks. The "country style" kitchen area was probably fashionable in 1982, when it was installed, but today it was chipped and battered with one of the draw fronts missing completely and several handles superglued back on but never quite in their original position. A couple of photos from home decorated the living area and Manuela always picked fresh wildflowers whenever she took Alessandro out for a walk. Whatever time of year it was she always managed to find something to brighten the place up.

Claudio looked around and tried to remember when claustrophobia had taken the place of romance.

"How about I make us a Melanzane alla Parmigiana?" Manuela was turning a fat aubergine in her hand. "We'll have a nice dinner together before you go off to work. You watch Allessandro while I make it." She deposited their six month old on the sofa bed next to Claudio.

Claudio grunted acceptance then watched her for a while as she set about preparing dinner. Her long dark hair had been cut short since she'd had Allessandro, for convenience she said. He missed running his fingers through her hair, it was one of the first things he'd noticed about her on their very first date.

Claudio turned his attention to Allessandro and smiled. If the apartment had been small for two people it was miniscule for three. It wasn't the size of the baby that was the problem it was size of the things that came with him; toys, changing mats, nappies and bottles filled every available space. Despite Claudio's best efforts Allessandro's dark brown eyes barely left Manuela as she swished around the kitchen expertly chopping vegetables and juggling an array of pots and pans.

"What's the event tonight?" she asked.

"Just some corporate bash for a bunch of overpaid lawyers." Claudio jiggled a rattle in front of Alessandro

"Maybe you should talk to some of them, they may know someone, they're the sort of people that like a nice wine."

We're not allowed to talk to them, I just have to serve them some food and keep out of their way."

"What's the worst that could happen? Just try chatting to one of them, you never know."

"I could lose my job, that's the worst that could happen, and then how do you think we'd eat?" snapped Claudio. He handed the rattle to Allesandro, grabbed the remote control and started flicking through TV channels.

They had big plans once; Claudio was going to set up a business importing wine from his parent's vineyard in the heart of Tuscany, to small, chic, cafe bars and restaurants across the north of England while Manuela continued her rise through the ranks at the large supermarket where she worked as a purchaser. But things didn't quite work out that way.

She fell pregnant just a few months after they arrived in England and with such a short service record there was no enhanced maternity leave. There were no friends or family living locally to help out and with professional childcare costs being so high they'd agreed that Claudio would take on extra work to make ends meet. Manuela stayed home with the baby and took what agency work she could as a translator, but in reality it was slim pickings in a very competitive market. They often talked about returning home but to what? Claudio's pride wouldn't let them.

Manuela popped the dinner in the oven and opened a bottle of red wine. She poured herself a large glass and reached one for Claudio.

"Not for me, I'm working, remember?" he said flatly still staring at the TV.

She rolled her eyes and downed half her glass in a couple of large guilty gulps.

They could barely afford to eat, never mind save up to start a business. Claudio had taken a temporary contract in the kitchen of a big Carlisle hotel, hoping to work his way up: "If the General Manager of The Dorchester Hotel in London could work his way up from a wine waiter, then so can I" he was fond of saying. The shifts were rarely convenient but the money and the tips were good and, in a field where casual labour could not usually be relied upon to deliver the all important service to the customer, Claudio stood out and was soon offered a permanent contract.

They sat on the sofa with dinner on their knees watching TV and not speaking to each other. Lives played out across the screen as people fussed and worried over the perfect house to buy. Did any of them truly realise how lucky they were? He would have loved any one of the houses the spoiled contestants were busy turning their noses up at. Choice was a luxury he could not afford. Alessandro gurgled and laughed in his play pen on the floor. When Claudio got up to leave for work Manuela grabbed his arm and hugged him tight.

"Stay safe *tesoro* – you know that I love you, don't you?" she said, stepping back to look at him.

"I know," he replied, not meeting her gaze.

"Don't give up just yet – there's still so much we could do."

"I know."

"There's a business administration course at the college starting in September and they have a crèche so I could study and learn the business skills we need."

"We'll see."

"Just think about it." She twisted her neck to try and meet his gaze "You know we need to find a way out of this." She reached up and kissed him on the cheek.

Claudio finally turned and looked at her. A fiery spark of determination flickered behind her tired eyes. He sighed, saying nothing, then "I'm sorry. I'm so tired with all the extra shifts and still we're getting nowhere. I should be providing for my family, not living like this." He gestured around the room.

"I can live with this," replied Manuela, repeating his gesture. "So long as I have you."

"Why do you put up with me?" he asked, smiling as he brushed the hair away from her eyes. "Look, I'll try talking to someone and do my best not to get fired. We'll be fine anyway with a big shot business woman in the house."

She laughed and he held her close, kissing the top of her head. "Don't forget it's us versus the world, not us versus each other." she whispered.

"I'll text you when my shift ends," he said stepping back. "And don't forget to warm up my side of the bed." He smiled as he grabbed his coat and headed out of the door.

At the hotel the corporate event was the same as all the others he'd worked at; posh frocks and polite conversation descending into kicked off shoes and increasingly vulgar jokes as the self congratulatory speeches droned on. As the wine went down the volume went up. Everyone was nice enough but most of them ignored him as he hurried around serving their meals.

Towards the end of the evening one rather tipsy lawyer in a navy pinstripe suit and waistcoat waved him over. "Old school," thought Claudio.

"Are you Italian?" he asked. "You look Italian." he added, before Claudio had chance to answer.

"Yes sir I am Italian."

"I'm learning to speak Italian – can I practice on you?"

"Of course."

The lawyer cleared his throat, looked Claudio in the eye and said with a flourish "Grazie per la cena, ero ottima!" He gesticulated in an exaggerated fashion to emphasise his point.

Claudio laughed and the lawyer looked hurt "What did I say wrong?"

"I think you mean 'era ottima' not 'ero' – you just told me 'thank you for dinner, I was fabulous!'"

The lawyer roared with laughter. "Wait until I tell them that one in my evening class – that past tense will really be the death of me! So what are you doing waiting tables?" he asked "You speak two languages fluently – there must be something you can do with that?"

"I speak three actually," replied Claudio. "My mother is Spanish and the languages are really very similar." He looked at the lawyer, weighing him up; he seemed OK and, judging by the non-regulation bottle of wine in front of him, he appreciated a decent vintage. "My parents own the vineyard next door to where that bottle was produced," he said, pointing to the empty bottle of

Lamole di Lamole Chianti Classico on the table. "I grew up on a vineyard in Lamole and hope one day to import my parent's wine into the UK but I've not had a lot of luck so far."

"Amazing! I was in Lamole just last year, we visited for the Chianti Wine Festival and took a drive to check out the smaller vineyards. Had an amazing Bistecca di Fiorentina at the bistro up there."

"My cousin's bistro." Claudio grinned. "Did you see the dog?"

"I did! Lovely thing! He sniffed around our feet from the moment we arrived! Sit down!" said the lawyer gesturing to the seat next to him. "I'm Henry – let's see if I can't find a way to help you, I have a lot of wine swilling friends and they're always after a good new bottle to try, between us we should be able to sort something out."

The party was breaking up and it was only 10 minutes to the end of his shift. Claudio knew his boss was likely to be busy behind the scenes so, taking his chances, he pulled up the chair next to Henry. They were soon deep in conversation about the relative merits of the many Tuscan vineyards, the specialist butcher who served every kind of wild boar meat available and what the secrets were behind a really good grape.

"I'm sorry sir, is this waiter bothering you?"

Claudio turned to see Mark, his boss, stood right behind him. "Porca miseria! Dammit!" he muttered, standing up. "I...erm...this gentleman..." His voice tailed off. Henry intervened.

"Are you the manager around here? Excellent! I was just chatting to this fine waiter about your Christmas functions. Do you have a leaflet or something I could look at?"

"Of course sir," replied Mark with a practiced smile. "Claudio, go and fetch this gentleman one of our Christmas brochures and please hurry."

Claudio flashed a grateful smile at Henry and scampered off to the office for the brochure. When he returned Mark and Henry were still talking.

"Here you go sir." Claudio handed the brochure to Henry.

"And here you go," replied Henry, handing Claudio a five pound note. "Thank you for looking after us all so well this evening and I very much enjoyed our conversation." Henry looked pointedly into Claudio's eyes.

"Thank you. That's very generous of you sir." Claudio returned to his locker and opened the five pound note, inside was a note. "Meet Thin White Duke 10 mins. H." Claudio smiled and leaned his head against his locker with a relieved sigh. He quickly changed out of his work clothes and fired off a text to Manuela before he hurried out to join Henry.

"You were right; I think I've found someone who can really help us. Might be a little later than planned, but it will be worth it. Love you both. Xx"

He slipped the phone into his pocket, grabbed his bag and raced around to the nearby bar where he easily found Henry with two larges glasses of grappa ready and waiting.

"Glad you got my message," smiled Henry. "I told your boss I was making notes about the Christmas party! Now, I have a big dinner party coming up for my wife's 50th; I've invited a bunch of very influential friends and I want to impress them all with the wine list." The hotel Christmas brochure was in a sticky puddle on the bar and Henry was using it as a coaster. "I'd like you to source and supply all the wines for me – how does that sound? I should warn you, they all think they're wine buffs and they can all drink plenty so we'll be keeping you nice and busy. Are you up for it?"

Claudio reached into his jacket for his notebook. "No problem at all sir," he smiled. "Where would you like to start?"

CARLISLE – IN REAL LIFE

There are few cities with a more fascinating history than Carlisle. Over the centuries it has seen more than its fair share of battles and sieges and this history can be fully explored both in the castle and in Tullie House Museum (which also has a fine cafe). In addition to this there are also some lovely walks along the river and, on a sunny afternoon, Bitts Park is the perfect place for a picnic.

Carlisle's other claim to fame is that it is home to the original Carr's biscuit factory. It was founded in 1831 and their famous water biscuits were an instant hit, so much so that within 15 years it was the largest bakery in Britain. Over recent years it has been taken over by McVities but the original factory is still there (albeit with a few modern additions) and we all held our breath when it was flooded by Storm Desmond in 2015. Fortunately it was just a few months until production of ginger nuts and bourbon creams resumed.

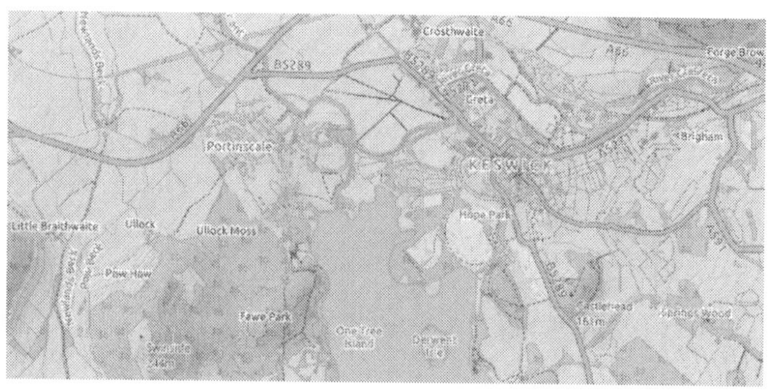

EVERYONE'S A WINNER

Laura licked the doughnut sugar from the corner of her mouth as a small blob of jam crept down her chin.

"You missed a bit," laughed Emily, pointing to her own chin to show where it was.

Laura picked up the napkin from the table and wiped her chin.

"Other side."

Laura tried again, this time clearing the offending jammy blob. "That'll teach me, I really shouldn't have had that. Heaven knows how many Slimming World Syns there were in it!"

"Who cares?" said Emily, poring over the map. "We've got another 2 miles ahead of us and that's on top of the 8 we've already done."

She put the map to one side, fiddled around with the string on the top of her well packed rucksack, gently pressing her neatly folded top down inside so it didn't catch on the toggle. She leaned the rucksack against the table leg then tidied their plates away onto the empty tray and wiped the crumbs off the table with her napkin before returning the map to the table.

Laura peered out through the steamed up windows of the cafe into the slow drizzle of the late afternoon, the mist from the windows indistinguishable from the clouds beyond. She pulled her chair in to let someone squeeze past "Why do they always cram the tables so close together?" she muttered. "I've barely got room to breathe here!"

Emily smirked. "You putting your waterproofs back on?"

"Nah, too hot. Well, maybe the top, but not the legs. How hilly is the next section?"

"All flat." replied Emily.

Laura sighed, screwing up her nose as she peered out of the window again. "How about we just give it 5 more minutes to see if it clears up?"

Emily clenched her jaw with irritation and wondered why Laura had agreed to come on the hike when all she'd done was complain about the weather. She'd been in an odd mood all morning. Emily watched as she tipped half the contents of her rucksack onto the floor of the cafe and rummaged through them looking for a hair band. Locating one she slipped it on, pushing her loose blonde hair back off her face. "That's better," she smiled, haphazardly stuffing the contents back in and pulling the lid down tight. "Damn! Forgot my hat!" she muttered before repeating the entire process again.

Emily thought back to the networking event where they'd met just 2 weeks earlier. They'd really clicked and had kept in touch with texts and messages since then. Their shared love of hiking led Emily to suggest a 10 mile yomp around Derwent Water; it had been glorious weather when they planned it but today was the first dismal day in ages.

Glancing at the floor Emily noticed a small box half under Laura's chair. "You missed something," she said, using her foot to slide it closer before bending to pick it up. She handed it over to Laura. Clear Blue Pregnancy Testing Kit. "Anything you want to tell me?" asked Emily, smiling.

Laura's face flushed. They'd only known each other such a short time. Emily reached over and put her hand on Laura's arm. "Honestly, just blurt it out, I promise you can trust me."

Laura hesitated, biting her lower lip and searching Emily's face for some sign of reassurance.

"Well, it's like this," she finally began. "We've been trying for kids for a little while and I think I may actually be pregnant, except now it's finally real I am absolutely terrified. I haven't even told Pete. I bought the test before I met you in Keswick earlier, but I'm too scared to use it. I'm scared I might be pregnant and equally scared that I might not be; does that make any sense at all?"

"Sort of a Schrödinger's baby scenario?" said Emily.

Laura laughed "Exactly; if I don't take the test then I am both pregnant and not pregnant at the same time."

"What are you scared of?" asked Emily, her hand still resting on Laura's arm and her hazel eyes never leaving her face.

"Everything!" blurted Laura. "I just don't feel grown up enough to look after a baby. I've killed every houseplant I've ever owned!"

"Babies are different," said Emily reassuringly. "For a start you can't leave them on windowsills unattended and I'm pretty sure you need to water them more than once a week."

They both laughed.

"Seriously though," she continued, "You *can* do this; millions of women have done it before you and there will be loads of people around to support you – Pete, your family, the nurses, your friends, me."

"I know, I'm being silly."

"Not silly at all, this is the biggest change you'll ever make in your life. Of course you'll be nervous, but you've got this; whatever the result of that test you'll cope just fine."

Laura smiled and put her hand on top of Emily's. "Thank you. I just need to take a deep breath and pull myself together."

"Tell you what," said Emily, "When we get back to Keswick we'll nip to the public loos in Booth's and do it. I'll be right outside the whole time."

"Deal!"

As they trudged their way back into Keswick they talked about a million different things and none of them were baby related. Crossing the bridge back into town Laura stopped again.

"I can't do this. I am so scared!"

"Wait there 2 minutes," instructed Emily, disappearing off into the nearby CoOp. She emerged soon after clutching a small bottle of Shiraz and a scratch card.

"This is for Dutch courage," she said, waving the wine bottle. "And this," waving the scratch card, "is to give me something to do while you're in there."

Giggling like naughty school children they drank the wine straight from the bottle and raced to Booth's before Laura changed her mind again.

"Right," said Emily "In you go. I'll wait out here and see how many millions we've won."

Laura disappeared into the cubicle while Emily dug 2p out of her purse and started on her scratch card.

"You ok?" she called through

"Yup, just got to wait 2 minutes now."

"Can you remember the Countdown music?" They both began giggling and humming together, finishing with a flourishing "did-di, did-di, diddly bum!"

"Well?" asked Emily

"Negative," said Laura, opening the cubicle door.

"Same here; it would seem that we are neither pregnant nor millionaires. How are you feeling?"

"I'm OK actually," said Laura, her voice muffled in Emily's shoulder as she gave her a big hug. "Thanks for being there."

"No worries," Emily smiled. "What shall I do with these?" They looked around for a bin, but there was none.

"There's a sanitary bin next to the loo." Said Laura "It's not perfect but we may as well just leave them there."

"Fair enough," said Emily, placing the lottery ticket, the empty wine bottle and the pregnancy test on top of the bin next to the toilet.

"I think after all that we deserve a larger glass of wine; the Dog and Gun do great food too – you in?"

"Definitely!" smiled Laura as they made their way outside and the first rays of weak sunshine finally broke through the clouds.

DERWENT WATER – IN REAL LIFE

This story was inspired by a real "still life" that I discovered, although I have changed the location. A lap of Derwent Water is a great day hike with the added benefit that if you get tired along the way you can always take one of the launches back to the start.

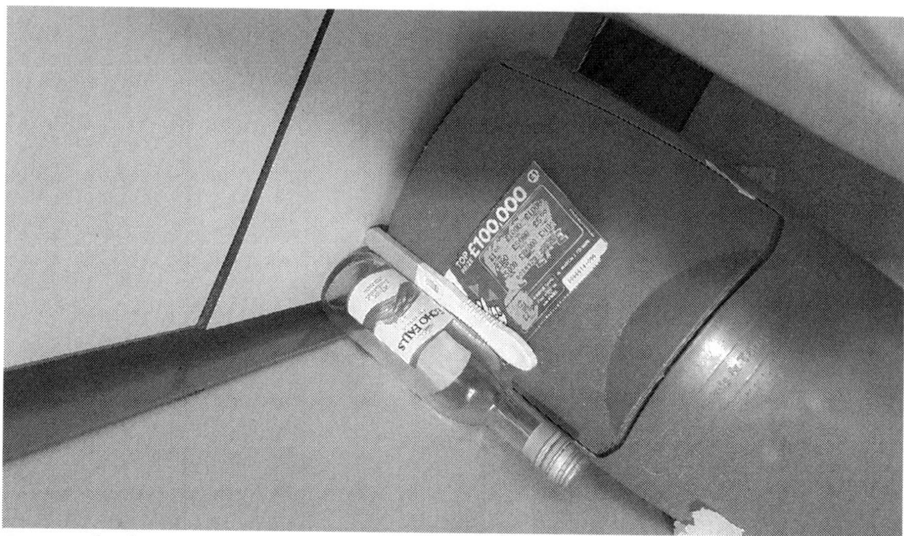

Several thousand years ago Derwent Water and Bassenthwaite Lake were all one lake and, during times of flood, they pretty much still are today. If you're planning a lap of the lake after a period of wet weather do be prepared for boggy ground and maybe even the odd paddle; catchment area for the lake is the surrounding high fells and the lake levels can vary dramatically.

There are a few hotels and bars along the eastern shore but nothing along the western shore until you get to Portinscale where you'll find and excellent pub and the Chalet Cafe, which is the cafe where we begin the story.

Printed in Great Britain
by Amazon